MW01170827

TEXTUAL RELATIONS

TEXTUAL RELATIONS

Jamie Lee Scott

LBB Company
United States of America

LBB Company
1106 Hwy 69 N
Forest City, IA 50436

ISBN-13: 978-1480159556 ISBN-10: 1480159557

Manufactured in the United States of America

10 9 8 7 6 5 4 3 2 1

Acknowledgements

As with any novel, there are so many people to thank. There are so many people without whom this text wouldn't exist. I've listed just a few of them here.

Scot Dierks, again, thanks for being the most understanding and supportive husband a woman could ask for, in so many ways. And thanks for letting me attempt to live my dream.

Teresa Watson, editor extraordinaire. Thanks for the last minute revisions, the advice, the support, and for making Textual Relations a better book. Thanks for taking time away from your own endeavors to help me with mine.

To my beta readers: Bente Gallagher (also known as New York Times bestselling author Jennie Bentley) and Stacy Jeziorowski for taking early looks, making suggestions, and for being the best fans.

Lastly, to Martin Crosbie, who helped push me to the next level. I can't even tell you how much he's done for so many people.

CHAPTER 1

Getting started in the mornings has always been hard for me. I hit my snooze button at least three times. Even Lola, my Doberman, isn't fooled by the alarm anymore. She doesn't even stir until she hears me press the reset button, which means I'm finally getting up.

When the damn thing screamed at me for the third time that morning, I rolled over to press reset. I got about halfway to the clock on my nightstand when the covers that had tangled around my body in my apparently restless sleep threatened to cut me in half. The shrill sound pierced the air for so long, Lola began howling. I wrestled the satin sheets from around my middle and threw the covers to the floor.

Lola immediately pounced on the covers, rolled over on her back, and wriggled in an attempt to scratch her back. I slammed my hand down on the clock hard enough to break it. Ah, silence.

I'm Mimi Capurro, owner of Gotcha Detective Agency in Salinas, California. My business is fledgling, but since news of our involvement in catching a murderer hit the presses, business has been picking up.

The aforementioned murder occurred when I was working as a bodyguard for *New York Times* bestselling author, Lauren Silke. The victim was her assistant, who I was *not* protecting. I got involved in the case, and as luck (or skill) would have it, we caught the killer. I feel bad that such a nice girl had to die, and we got great PR from a bad situation, but let's face it: detective work is "bad situation" business.

I picked up the blankets Lola had been rolling on and tossed them in the washer on my way to the bathroom.

My house is more like a small cottage, so everything is close together, and my stackable washer and dryer happened to be in the closet outside the bathroom. I stuffed the blankets in, but didn't turn it on, because I felt it was more important for me to have water pressure for my shower than to get the blankets cleaned.

I looked at my watch as I got undressed. Shit, I'd really slept in. Instead of enjoying a leisurely shower, I jumped in, shampooed, rinsed, and conditioned in less than five minutes. No time to shave my legs, so I'd have to wear pants.

Lola was scratching at the back door by the time I'd finished putting on my eyeliner and mascara, so I dabbed on my nude lip stain as I headed out the door.

By the time I arrived at the Victorian house that is home to Gotcha Detective Agency, Lola was frothing at the mouth. I was late, and she had a strict schedule. She must have her morning snack from Charles Parks, one of my detectives, by 8:30am. We were only five minutes late. She scratched at the passenger window when I parked in the lot, so I leaned across my Land Rover, opened the passenger door, and as soon as I grabbed the handle, Lola pushed hard against the door and flew across the yard to the kitchen door.

I looked in the rearview mirror and checked my makeup. Today I went for minimal, with just foundation, blush, liner and mascara. Oh, and a bit of lip stain too, so I didn't look dead. I'd dressed in a black turtleneck and slacks, my usual business casual, and I had my hair pulled up into a high ponytail, which I swear takes five years off my looks.

When I finally got out of the car, Charles stood outside the door, hand-feeding Lola her treats. As I walked up the steps, he put his finger to his lips.

"Huge fight going on in there. If we're quiet, maybe we can catch the rest before they realize everyone can hear them." Charles grabbed Lola's collar and led her into my office.

When he came back into the kitchen, we stood quiet and still. I knew the voices, but I'd never heard them at this level.

"When you make enough money to pay the mortgage and buy food, then you can do whatever you want. But until then, you live under my roof, and it's my rules," Jackie Baccarin, another of my detectives and my best friend, screamed.

"That's so unfair. It's my computer." That whining voice belonged to Jackie's fourteen-year-old daughter, Catey.

"Get over it. Life is unfair," Jackie said. There was a slamming noise. "And it's not your computer, it's mine. I paid for it, and I let you use it. If you don't give me the passwords, then you won't be using it anymore."

"Fine, I don't care. I'll just use Amanda's computer. Her mom lets her have her computer in her bedroom. She's not a control freak like you."

"Well, good for Amanda! When she starts smoking dope in her bedroom, maybe her mom can join her." Jackie must have stood quickly, because I heard her chair hit the wall. "We're done here, young lady. Not only are you not going to have your own computer until I have all the passwords, you're grounded until further notice."

"Until further notice?" Catey sounded flabbergasted. "You can't do that. You have to give me a time."

"I don't have to do anything. Now you'd better get a move on, because I won't be writing you a note if you're late for school."

"No. It's my civil right to know the term of my punishment," Catey snapped.

"As long as you live in my house, you have no civil rights," Jackie stated in a matter-of-fact tone. "Go. School. Now."

We watched as Catey, dressed in school regulation black pants and white oxford shirt, stormed out of the building.

I looked at Charles. "So, what's the scoop?"

Charles's face went slack. No more morning drama for him. He walked over to the coffee machine. "Want some?"

"I could use the caffeine. Late stakeout last night." I plopped down at the kitchen table.

"I guess Jackie is suspicious of some of Catey's behavior lately, so she asked her for the passwords to her laptop, and all of her social networking accounts. Catey refused, so Jackie brought Catey's laptop in for me to try to figure out the passwords." Charles poured coffee as he spoke.

He walked to the table, handed me my coffee cup, and sat down across from me. "The Internet is such a dangerous place for teens," I said, after my first sip.

"Jackie no sooner walked in the door when Catey stormed in behind her."

"Catey's not old enough to drive. How did she get here?"

Charles wrapped his hands around his cup as if he was cold. "I guess her best friend's mom dropped her off."

Before we could finish our conversation, Gemma Olivetti, my junior detective, peeked into the kitchen. "Mimi, you have a visitor."

Gemma was still that age where miniskirts were appropriate, and she flaunted it. The tight beige skirt and even tighter monochrome shirt would have looked ridiculous on anyone older, or less fit. Gemma wore it like a second skin she'd lived in all her life.

"Who is it?" I wasn't ready to see people yet. I hadn't even finished my coffee.

"I didn't even ask his name," Gemma said, perplexed. "It's just that he's so freaking hot, he caught me off guard when he asked for *you*."

I raised my brows. "Excuse me?"

"I mean, usually when the guy at the front desk is that sexy, he's asking for Charles." She looked at Charles and winked.

"Maybe he *is* here for me. You know Charles and Mimi sound similar. Are you sure you aren't mistaken?" Charles stood before I did.

I wasn't even out of my seat before Charles sprinted toward reception. Good, I'd have a minute or two before I had to deal with the day. I'd barely gotten my cup rinsed out when Charles was back.

"You are *not* going to believe who's here."

Before I could guess, a tall man, dressed in a white oxford shirt and navy slacks, entered the kitchen. He took my breath away. Part of it was his good looks, but part of it was that I never expected to see him again. We just didn't run in the same circles, as he was a computer whiz, and I could barely open a can of Cheese Whiz.

"Sebastian," I breathed. "What are you doing here?"

It had been a few months since I'd seen him. He was the boyfriend, or rather ex-boyfriend, of the girl that had been murdered. Sebastian was indeed sexy, and I could see how even the luscious Gemma would be taken aback by him, but he was also a bit scary. His dark wavy hair and tanned skin only made his blue eyes that much more blue. To keep myself from getting too hormonal, I tried to remember the details of the sleeve of tattoos covering his arms. When he pushed up his sleeves, the blanket of ink reminded me that we came from very different worlds.

"It's been awhile." His genuine smile beamed. "I thought since things have settled a bit, maybe we could talk."

I looked over to Charles, giving him the "I've got it from here" look, dismissing him. Being Charles, he completely ignored me.

"Sebastian, how goes the game?" Charles poured himself another cup of coffee. He was settling in.

"We had to call it quits for a bit. The PR campaign sort of fell apart after the murder and all. But Henry, Eugene and I have a meeting next week." Sebastian looked back to me. "Is there a place we can talk?"

I looked at Charles, who was thoroughly enjoying my discomfort.

Sebastian was not only the ex-boyfriend of the murder victim, he had been a suspect. Among other things, he was also quite fond of me for some reason.

Since he was at least ten years younger than me, I never took him seriously.

"Let's go into my office." I poured more coffee into the cup I'd just rinsed, so I could have something to do with my hands. "Coffee?"

"No, thanks."

I walked to my office and felt like a huge shadow was hanging over me. Did I mention Sebastian was more than six feet tall?

I sat at my desk and motioned for him to take a chair on the other side. It hadn't been that long since his dead ex-girlfriend had been sitting in that same chair. He sat, and I felt better with the desk between us. I couldn't imagine why he was here.

"Okay, this is going to sound, I don't know, stalkerish." Sebastian wasn't his normal cocky self.

"Stalkerish?" I asked.

"Look, I'm just going to say this, and don't interrupt me, or I won't get through it."

"Okay." Oops.

"I've been thinking about you ever since you came to see me that day. I know the timing was bad, and I should never have been so forward with you. Then the whole alibi thing and sex with Esme, and Susan, and then, uh, Esme. I just want you to know, I've forced myself to wait this long to come see you. I'm not a creep, I'm not crazy, and I know the tattoos and the vampire thing sort of put you off, but I'm really a nice guy. Sure, I was a bit full of myself about the girls, but you are a woman." Sebastian was rambling.

"Wait." I stood up. "Just wait a minute. Why exactly are you here?"

"I want you to have lunch with me," Sebastian blurted out.

"No, no, no. I thought we talked about this. I'm so much older than you, and I'm not looking for a boyfriend." I walked around my desk to show him the door.

Sebastian stood. "It's not like that. I haven't been with anyone since that day. And it's just lunch."

I wanted to be flattered, but I was grossed out by the fact that he had sex with Esme the night she died. Then again, who was I to judge? I wasn't perfect, and I'd had sex with more than one man in my life. Truth be told, I was flattered.

"Just lunch?" Was I really giving in that easily?

"Just lunch between friends," Sebastian said. "We can see if maybe you might be able to really like me."

I had to laugh. He had no idea what he was getting into. "And maybe, you'll stop liking me."

He laughed. "So it's a date? When and where?"

I looked over at my desk. I didn't want to go through my Blackberry and "fit him in" so I said, "Leave me your card and I'll call you. I'll know more about my schedule after our morning staff meeting."

Sebastian pulled his wallet from his pocket and slipped a business card out. He handed it to me, and then leaned over and kissed me on the cheek. "Thanks. I'm really looking forward to it."

I stood frozen in place and watched Sebastian walk out of my office.

As soon as the front door closed, Charles arrived in my office. Close on his heels was a frazzled looking Jackie.

"Wait until I tell Nick," Charles purred.

Nick, or rather Detective Nick Christianson, was the homicide cop from the murder we investigated.

Nick also happened to be my college playmate, as in we had sex but weren't dating. It ended badly.

"What on earth would you tell Nick for?" If he told Nick, I'd kill him. I didn't care if I'd have to hire another computer forensics expert.

"He always said Sebastian had the hots for you." Charles sat in the same chair Sebastian had just vacated. "Oh, I can still feel him."

Jackie stood there, silent, which was very uncharacteristic of my friend.

"So Jackie, do we need to have a powwow?" I wanted to focus on something else and this was perfect.

Jackie sat on the chair next to Charles. "I'm so sorry about the yelling. Thank goodness we didn't have any clients in this morning."

Jackie had been my friend since we were kids. We had been through a lot together. When I looked at her sitting there, she looked more stressed than I'd ever seen her. Believe me, I've seen her stressed. I was there when her skanky ex-husband left her. She'd been quite a bit heavier then. The best thing to ever happen, next to having her kids, was Bradley leaving her. She got her confidence back, lost weight, and came to work for me. She's now the epitome of fashion for women over 30. Today, she wore skinny jeans with layered t-shirts in pastels of violet, blue and grey. The colors looked good with her pale skin and red hair.

"I'm not remotely worried about the yelling. I'm worried about you and Catey."

She leaned forward and put her face in her hands. "She's been acting weird lately."

"Weird? In what way?"

"She doesn't go out with her friends as much. She stays in her room with the door closed, and is either texting or typing away on her computer." Jackie looked up. "It's just not like her."

Charles had changed moods considerably. "So you took her laptop and cell phone. Good for you."

"That's what the fight was about. She wouldn't give me the passwords, so I took them. I didn't sneak them away. I told her exactly what I was doing." She sat back in the chair and ran her fingers through her hair.

I looked at her messed up bangs and wanted to straighten them, but it was just a distraction from the situation at hand. I hated to get involved in family matters. Well, wait, that's what I do for a living: I follow cheating spouses. Never mind.

"Where's the computer?" Charles asked. "Let me take a look at it."

"Hold up there, Wiley Coyote. Let's get the whole story, so you know what you are looking for," I said.

Jackie looked at me. "I think she's been talking to a boy online. I mean like sexting him."

"What the hell?" *Sexting*, was that even a word?

Charles looked at me like I was a six-year-old. "It's the new phone sex. They text each other dirty messages, pictures, and whatnot."

I was immediately intrigued and repulsed. "So how do you know they were sexting if you can't get past the passwords?"

"She had a picture I didn't recognize as her wallpaper on her phone. It was a really cute boy, but no one I knew. When I asked her who he was, she got defensive. I mean really defensive. Then she stopped leaving her laptop open, and every time I open it, it asks for a password. I've tried everything."

Charles leaned in close to Jackie and asked, "Have you thought about the possibility that it's an older boy she's texting and talking to?"

I could see Jackie holding her breath, trying not to cry. "I tried to talk to her about it, you know, ask what his name was, how old he was, but she shut down on me. She's always shared with me. So I asked Corey. He said not to worry; they haven't even talked on the phone or anything. He said she met him on a social site. I guess they have a lot of mutual friends, and he's interested in the same things she is."

Corey is Catey's twin brother.

"Red flag," Charles said quietly.

"Huge red flag," Jackie agreed. "But then I thought, maybe I'm just being a paranoid mom. Last night, I laid awake in bed and thought about what could happen to my daughter, as if I wasn't paranoid enough. So I brought the computer and Catey's phone to work."

Charles's computer forensics work is sought after, even by the Naval Postgraduate School in Monterey, so he's our man for this kind of job. On cases like this, Charles's computer skills save us from a wild goose chase.

Charles and I stood at the same time. "Let's go take a look," I said.

"Better yet, why don't I take a look, and I'll let you know what I come up with. I do better without a couple of hens pecking at me while I work." Charles headed out without waiting for an answer.

"Are you going to be okay?" I could see the fear in Jackie's eyes.

"Depends on what Charles comes up with. If it's just a simple teenage crush with a boy from Wisconsin, I'm good. I'm not even going to think about the alternative. Oh, Mimi, you're so lucky you don't have kids."

I didn't know about lucky. The reason I didn't have kids was because my husband died. I was barely used to the idea of being married when he went on a business trip and his plane crashed. He and the people he was with were never found. The wreckage spanned several miles, so finding parts was nearly impossible.

Not that I was planning a family even when Dominic was still alive. Lord knows his mother asked me about it every chance she got. I was pretty sure if she'd gotten a hold of my birth control pills, she'd have switch them for sugar pills. She wanted grandkids, and Dominic was her only child. Strange for an Italian family to only have one child, but apparently Dominic was a miracle baby.

My heart still aches every day, knowing the crash was so bad there weren't even pieces to bury. I can't imagine how his mom handles it. And I'm not in a place to ask either, since his family has broken all contact with me.

"I don't know about that. Maybe someday things will work out for me and I'll be in a situation to have a family." I sat back at my desk and sipped my coffee, which was lukewarm now.

"I'm sorry, Mimi, that was insensitive. I didn't mean it like that." Jackie looked on the verge of tears.

"Don't worry about it. I'm not even in the market for a boyfriend, much less a family." I laughed. And I meant it. I was good with where my life was.

I wasn't about to admit that the thought of Nick and I getting nearly naked on my couch flashed in my mind daily. It had been months since Charles, and his primo timing, had interrupted Nick and I in the throes of passion. And I was better for it. Even though I could still feel Nick on top of me when I thought about it, it was best that we never got further than a make out session.

"Speaking of boyfriends, have you talked to Nick lately?"

This was a conversation I didn't want to have. Since Jackie was my friend from high school, she'd been around when Nick and I had our "thing." She'd kept telling me that I couldn't have sex without getting my heart broken. I kept telling her I was fine. I wasn't fine, and Nick and I parted ways our junior year of college. Even though his NFL career kept him in the news, we never kept in contact, so it was a shocker when he turned out to be the homicide detective on the Esme Bailey murder case.

"Nope." I tried to sound casual. "We did work well together on that case, but it was strictly professional. And since I haven't come across any dead bodies lately, there's no reason for us to see each other."

"You know there's more to it than that." Jackie knew me too well.

"Not so much. Besides, I have a lunch date. A real date, mind you." I grinned. I thought about lunch with Sebastian. I would be a cougar.

Jackie stood. "Who?"

"Sebastian." She knew who he was, though she'd never met him.

"The creeper from the vampire murder?" She grabbed my cup. "Come on. Let's eat something while we're waiting for Charles."

"He's not a creeper," I said, as I followed her to the kitchen. I wasn't sure why I felt the need to defend him.

Jackie rummaged through the kitchen cabinets and pulled out some crackers, peanut butter, and honey. I refilled my coffee cup and poured a cup for her.

She smeared peanut butter on the crackers and licked the excess off the knife. "Well, Charles likes him, but that doesn't mean anything. I thought his involvement with those two girls was a bit gross. I mean having sex with two girls who lived together? Yuck."

"He's young," I said, by way of defense.

"Oh, that's a good reason to bang best friends." Jackie sat the plate of crackers on the table.

I looked at them longingly, wanting to eat every cracker, but then I looked down at my hips. I'm pretty sure I gained at least ten pounds in the last couple of months. Hoping and waiting for a phone call will make a girl eat more than she should. What I should have done was spend those anxious minutes (okay, hours) running. One cracker, I told myself, I could have *one*.

As my luck would have it, Charles walked back into the room just as I stuffed the peanut butter goodness into my mouth. He didn't say anything, but his gaze lingered on my hips. I wanted to flip him off.

"There'd better be one on that plate for me." Charles reached out with his manicured hand and snatched up a cracker.

"Don't you dare put that in your mouth until you give me some information," Jackie snapped. She was serious, but there was a playful edge.

Charles's hand stopped midway to his mouth. He held the cracker there. "As a matter of fact…" He stuffed the cracker in his mouth, and I swear he purred.

"Bitch," Jackie said, and laughed.

Charles may be a fop, in his white Jeans and denim colored v-neck sweater that fit like a glove, but his manners didn't always keep up with his style. "You wish," he said around the peanut butter in his mouth. "But I do have a little something."

CHAPTER 2

I wasn't sure if I was relieved or more frustrated after Charles offered up his information. I understood it was the best he could do for the moment, but the waiting was killing me, so I could only imagine what it was doing to Jackie.

"I promise I'll have more by the end of the day." Charles grabbed another cracker. At this point, he was the only person eating.

Jackie said, "Please explain it to me one more time."

Charles actually swallowed before speaking. "Hacking the passwords was easy. I mean it's just the basic interface that came with the laptop. After I had that password, it was easy to hack into her email and social networking accounts. Once I was in, I found a series of emails and social posts from a guy named Dylan Frederick. I'm pretty sure it's not his real name. And by the way, your daughter needs to update her email provider to something more secure."

Impatient now, Jackie said, "I got that part. Thanks for writing down the passwords. I think I'll just give Catey back her laptop and phone, and tell her I changed my mind. She doesn't need to know you hacked in. But now what? I mean, I don't get the whole IP address thing."

Charles jumped up and sat on the kitchen counter. "The IP address is kind of like a P.O. box. It's a locator. Most people can only get the service provider information and maybe a city, if they're lucky." He put his fingers close to his mouth, breathed a fog on them, and polished them on his shirt. "But I can get you the exact location."

Jackie jumped up. "An exact location? So I can see where this boy lives? Oh, God, I hope it's a nice house in rural Wisconsin."

"What's with you and Wisconsin?" I asked.

"It's half way across the country, and only good boys come from farms in the Midwest, right?" Jackie sounded hopeful.

"Well, it's not Wisconsin. It's here in Salinas," Charles said.

Jackie slumped back down into her chair. "Shit." Then she sat up straight. "Well, maybe not so shitty. At least I can see who lives there. I mean, actually go to the address and see the boy."

"Not so fast, young lady." I had to interject. "You're a bit too close to this. Charles and I will go see who lives at the house. We can pretend we are census takers or something, ask who lives there."

"The census was taken a couple of years ago."

"Well, Charles, not everyone is as up on census taking as you are. We can fake it."

"Yes, we can," he agreed. "Jackie, you have work to do, so Mimi and I can take care of this. As soon as I have the address, we'll go check it out. Then you can do whatever you want with the information."

"I really think I should be doing this. It's my daughter, and you two already have plenty on your plates." Jackie stood again, this time clearing the dishes from the table.

"I don't think so." I stood too, and put my coffee cup in the sink. "You're too close to this, and if it turns out not to be a teenage boy Catey is flirting with, you may not be responsible for your actions."

"I'm level-headed." Jackie defended herself.

"Not according to the little tiff you had with your daughter this morning." Charles jumped down from the counter.

Just as he landed on his feet, Gemma came into the kitchen. "Did I miss anything?"

I'd forgotten all about the staff meeting. "No, but we aren't having our staff meeting this morning. Charles and I have to be someplace. Can you just give me a quick rundown of the cases you are working on?"

"Not fair. This is the first time I'm here for the new morning staff meetings and we aren't even having one?" Gemma had pouting down to a science. Damn if she didn't make pouting look sexy. Oh, to be that young again.

"I promise, tomorrow we'll have a meeting just for you. Now, what's on your agenda?"

Gemma smiled. "I'm process serving pretty much all day. That's about it. I do have a decoy job tomorrow night, though. I haven't done one of those in awhile. I'm really looking forward to it. I never get to flirt anymore."

Jackie said, "So, what do you call what you do with Charles every day?"

"Oh, that," Gemma laughed. "Torture."

Gemma feigned poking Charles in the belly, and he flinched away. It's not that he has an aversion to women, just Gemma. She loved to irritate Charles at every opportunity.

"Jackie, I need to have this week's records up to date before Friday, so why don't you get cracking on those while Charles and I are out? Then we'll see what to do from there."

Charles pulled his car keys from his pocket. "Be back in a bit."

I followed him out the back door. As much as I love my Land Rover, I loved being the passenger for a change. I climbed into the passenger seat of Charles's black Audi Spyder. This little sports car screamed sex, and Charles looked quite sexy behind the wheel.

"When will you have the information from the ISP?" I was feeling pretty cool for knowing that an Internet service provider was called ISP for short.

"I already have it. I don't need the ISP's permission to get the address. I just hacked in and got it myself." Charles outdid my smugness by leaps and bounds.

"Okay, but isn't that illegal?"

"And you started caring now?" Charles took his eyes off the road a bit too long for my taste as he glared at me.

"Fine. Jeez, watch where you're driving." I slouched down in my seat.

"I had the address, but I didn't want Jackie to know. I wanted to check out the house and see who lives there first. I'd rather go into this knowing what's in store. And I do know the owner of the house isn't Dylan Frederick."

"This isn't good." My heart felt sick.

"His name is William Garrison. My buddy at the academy was looking up his vitals. I have his cell phone number from Catey's phone."

"You wrote down all the passwords for Jackie, right?"

"Yes." Charles drew the word out.

"So she's going to be able to get into Catey's phone and read all the messages."

Charles reached into his front pocket. This was a feat, as he struggled around the seatbelt. It was only a moment before he handed me a cell phone.

"Catey's," Charles said.

"The password?"

Charles told me the password and within seconds, I was navigating through a very personal stream of text messages.

Dylan: *I really want a sundae, but I don't have ice cream. Can I pour chocolate on u lick until I get 2 ur cherry?*

Catey: *Haha, U R so cute. I'd love 2 have u lick chocolate off my body.*

The rest were in the same vein, until the very recent messages:

Dylan: *I can't stop thinking abt u. I need 2 c u.*

Catey: *I can't stop thinking of u either.*

Dylan: *What color panties r u wearing?*

Catey: *I'm not wearing any.*

Dylan: *Prove it.*

Catey: *Haha.*

Dylan: *I need 2 C u.*

Catey: *Call me.*

Dylan:*Seriously?*

Catey: *Call me.*

"Well?" Charles was getting impatient.

"Haven't you read them?"

"Of course I have. I just want to know what you think."

"I think that this is very sick. I mean phone sex is bad enough if you're an adult, but Catey is fourteen years old. She shouldn't even know this stuff." I could feel my stomach churning.

"Oh, honey, they learn a lot earlier these days. Sex is everywhere." Charles grabbed the phone and scrolled down. "See that?"

I looked at what he'd pointed out. I wasn't really sure what I was looking at. Then it hit me. We didn't need to know the IP location, the guy's address was in a text message. Holy shit. The text message was from two days ago.

"They were planning to meet up. I'm guessing they've either met, and he really is a teenage boy, or they haven't met and he's not a teen."

I didn't follow Charles's train of thought. "Why is that?"

"Well, Catey is acting like a typical teen. If she'd met up with this guy and he was a teen, she'd still be acting like a teen. If it was a man, she'd be acting a whole lot different." Charles was matter of fact.

I got it. She'd be humiliated if the "love of her young teen life" turned out to be a pedophile. All I could think was that Charles and I had to stop this before it went too far. I had no problem being the bad guy.

At that moment, I longed for the good old days, with no phones and no Internet. When I was a teenager, we met the guys we had crushes on in person. No texting. But there were some pretty long hours on the phone. I remember my mom footing the bill to put in what they called a "teen line." Then I just had to fight with my sister about phone use. And the greatest invention of all: call waiting. There weren't any predators pretending to be someone they weren't. It was all right there in front of you. Not anymore.

"Also, did you notice the texting stopped after she told him to call her?"

"So do you think that's the end of it?"

Charles laughed. "Hell no, now he's talking to her instead of texting. I just can't believe he'd text his address to her."

We rode the rest of the way in silence. I'm not sure what he was thinking, but I was ready to kill someone. I didn't care if it was a boy or a man. Catey was way too young for this kind of thing. Hell, I hadn't even French kissed a boy by the time I was Catey's age, and she was having sexting conversations. Gross.

Charles slowed the car. When we approached the house, he slowed even more, but didn't stop. He drove about a block down and parked on the street.

The neighborhood wasn't far from Jackie's house. I'd say less than a half-mile. It was a street of tract homes, all the same cookie cutter style, with only the paint color to differentiate one house from another. Most had the garages protruding from the front of the home, definitely an upper middle class area of town. These houses were well maintained with simple, well-manicured yards.

"You stay in the car. I'm going to take a look around the house. Maybe look in some windows and see if it looks like there is a teenage boy in the house."

"What if someone's home?" I was tense.

"I'm going to call the cell number and see if I hear ringing. If I get an answer, I'll know if anyone is home. If not, I may go snooping."

Charles walked away as if he was taking a casual stroll down the street. I sat in the passenger seat like a good girl. When Charles disappeared around the garage to the front door of the house, it took everything in my power to stay in the car. But I did because I didn't want to mess this up.

An hour and a half later (well it seemed like an hour and a half, but it was only ten minutes), Charles strolled right back up to the car. He got in and started the Spyder without saying a word.

I waited as long as I could stand it, and then asked, "Well?"

"I just don't know. Something about the house doesn't seem right. It looks very much like a bachelor pad, but I saw a backpack on the counter."

"What counter?" I was intrigued and wished I'd followed Charles.

"I went around to the backyard, and the curtains on the sliding glass door were wide open. I saw a laptop on the kitchen table, and a backpack on the counter. Only it looked like a girl's backpack, not a boy's."

"Not Catey's backpack?" My heart lurched in my chest.

"I'm pretty sure it's not. It was more like what a seven or eight-year-old might carry. You know, Harry Potter, or Twilight, something with that kind of design. I couldn't see it that well."

"What if Catey isn't the only girl he's 'courting'?" I didn't even want to think of this person with a girl younger than Catey.

"That's not our problem at the moment. Catey is our problem." Charles was very serious.

"But how much of a problem?" I asked it aloud, even though I knew the answer.

CHAPTER 3

Charles drove us back to the Gotcha offices. I sat quietly, contemplating our next move. He kept to the speed limit, but just barely, and I could feel him wanting to floor the accelerator. I kept quiet, because I really didn't know what to say. Who would explain to Jackie? I didn't want to be the one to tell her the news.

As he maneuvered the Spyder into a parking space in our lot, Charles said, "Let me do the talking. You'll probably say the wrong thing and get her too upset."

I wanted to argue with him, but I knew he was right. I got out of the car and walked into the building without saying anything. I went straight to my office, looking for Lola. She was just standing as I walked in. I had disturbed her nap.

I got down on my knees and hugged her around the neck. "I'm so glad you're just a baby, and that you're a dog. I'm not sure I could handle being a mom to a person." I kissed her on the lips.

When I let go of Lola, she shook her whole body as if she was shaking off water after a bath. Then she licked her lips and left the room. It's nice to be so loved.

Lola went to slurp some water while I went to my desk and called my mom.

"Hey, are you busy?" I asked.

My mom sounded harried as usual, like there is never enough time in a day. "Nope. What's up?"

"I'm working on a tough one, and I just wanted to call and say I love you." I'm not sure why this matter had me missing my mom, but I needed to tell her.

"Thanks babe, I love you, too. Is everything okay?" Her voice changed from harried to concern.

"Jackie's daughter has an online crush, and Charles and I were just looking into it for her." I took a breath. "Mom, I think I'm going to be sick."

"What on earth? What's going on?" Concern change to scared.

"We are pretty sure the online crush isn't a teenage boy."

"She's a lesbian? Oh, dear, who cares? It's all the rage these days." There was a bit of laughter in her words.

I had to laugh, even though I didn't really feel it. "No Mom, I'm sure no one would care about that. We think it's a man, not a boy, a man preying on a fourteen-year-old girl."

There was silence on the other end of the phone. "Mom?"

"Mimi, I just don't know what to say. I'm so glad I'm not raising kids in this day and age."

"I know. I'm not sure I ever want to have kids now. I'd want to shelter and protect them, but it's just not possible to be there all the time." My heart felt sick.

"I love you, Mimi. I'm going to call your sister and have a talk with her."

"Great idea, Mom. I love you, too." I hung up the phone and stared out the window.

My sister, Ann, has two kids, a boy and a girl. I was pretty sure they were getting to the age where Ann had to start worrying about this kind of crazy stuff. Mom would just mention what I was working on, and hopefully, Ann would get a hint and pay closer attention to what her kids were doing on their computers.

Jackie and Charles entered my office from the hallway. They moved like synchronized swimmers, each sitting and leaning forward in their chairs across from my desk. Somehow, this all felt so surreal.

"I wanted to tell Jackie everything with you in the room," Charles said to me.

"Go ahead." I braced myself to hear everything again.

Jackie sat quietly, but I could see her hands shaking.

"I want you to give Catey her phone back today. I'm not sure if you can get it to her by lunch."

Jackie looked at her watch. "I can do that."

"I've put a GPS tracking device in with the battery. She'll never know it's there." Charles took a deep breath. "Tell her you talked to us, and that we told you to trust her. Trust is so important in a family, and you want her to trust you, too."

"What?" Jackie looked pissed.

"I'll know where she is. But I want this guy to contact her. Something makes me think he's going to plan a meeting in the next couple of days."

"Who exactly is he?" Jackie started rocking.

"He's a grown man. I know where he lives, but I'm not going to tell you. If you stop him too soon, you'll just push him on to the next fourteen-year-old. I know your concern is for your daughter, but what if another mother was being selfish, and this is why this creep has moved on to Catey?"

I interrupted. "We need to stop him for good."

Charles glared at me. I sat back and shut up.

"I can't let Catey go too far. What if this guy seduces her? Did you see any of the text messages?"

Charles gripped the phone in his hand. He flipped it open and pushed a few buttons. "Do you really want to see them?"

"No," Jackie hesitated. "I mean yes, I want to see what this pervert has been saying to my baby girl."

Charles handed Jackie the phone. We watched her scroll through the messages.

"How do I delete these?" Jackie asked.

"You don't," Charles said. "She needs to think you were never able to get into her phone."

"Bullshit. I'm not leaving this porn on my baby's phone," Jackie said, barely above a whisper.

"Yes, honey, you are," I said. "I promise, as soon as he makes contact for a face to face meeting, we'll get him, and then we'll turn the phone over to the police. We need the evidence. Understand?"

Jackie dropped the phone into her lap and bowed her head. "This is the shit that happens to other people, not to me and my family."

Charles (who just so happens to be missing a sensitivity chip) said, "Wake up, Jackie. This is real life, and sometimes the shit hits our very own fans. We're just lucky that you're a smart and intuitive parent who noticed something was wrong. This is our chance to keep this from happening to anyone else."

I waited for a response, but Jackie said nothing.

"I'm going to call a friend and find out everything I can about this guy. I have his name, his cell phone number, and his address. That should be enough to find out a few other things. I'll let you know as soon as I have anything." Charles stood.

"Are we done here?" I asked.

"I am. Jackie needs to get over to the school and talk with Catey, so she has a chance to contact Dylan/William as soon as possible. The sooner a meeting is planned, the sooner we nail this pervert."

Jackie flipped her daughter's cell phone shut and stood. "Thanks so much, you two. I'm so lucky to have you as friends."

Jackie walked out of my office through the door that led to the kitchen. That meant she was leaving, because that was the fastest way to the parking lot. I'd never seen her so distraught.

"Oh, joy, this is going to be a fun case. And we aren't even making any money on it." He flicked imaginary lint from his white jeans. "I'm going to make sure the GPS is working on Catey's phone."

I tried to busy myself with paperwork and scheduling appointments, but my mind kept going back to Jackie and Catey. After a couple of hours, I couldn't take it anymore, so I got up and went to Charles's office.

When I peeked in the door, I could see he was intent on something. His office was smaller than mine, or maybe it just seemed smaller because he had so many gadgets in it. I had filing cabinets, and he had shelves of computer technology books, hacking devices, doohickeys and thingamabobs I couldn't even explain. His desk was on the far wall, and he chose to have his chair face the wall instead of the entrance, so I felt like I was sneaking up on him.

"What are you looking at?"

"Something is very wrong here." He pointed to his computer screen.

I could see a blip. It moved, stopped, and then moved again.

"If Jackie had given Catey back her phone, it would be pretty much stationary. The phone was at the school for less than ten minutes, and then it started moving. It's been following a weird pattern for over an hour."

"What does this mean?"

"Well, I think that either Catey left school right after her mom gave her back her phone, or Jackie never gave the phone to Catey at all." Charles pushed his blonde locks back with his fingers.

"Oh, shit," I said. Then Charles jumped up.

"Oh shit, is right. Fuck, I let her read the text messages. Remember what one of the last messages was?" Charles was now pacing in front of his computer screen.

"Come on. We gotta go." I grabbed Charles by the arm and he didn't resist.

CHAPTER 4

I could see Jackie sitting in the front seat of the Toyota pickup that Gotcha owned. She sat completely still, staring at the house. She didn't even move when Charles drove up behind the truck. I got out of the car before he shifted into park.

I walked up to the window of the Toyota and tapped. Jackie turned slowly to look at me, but she didn't roll down the window or make any move to get out of the car. I grabbed the door handle and opened the driver's door.

"You shouldn't have come here."

She looked at me as if in a daze. "I had to know." She looked back at the house.

"I went to give her back her phone, but she had left school." Jackie tried to stay calm, but her voice cracked. "She wasn't there." She burst into tears.

I leaned into the cramped space and held her. She wrapped her arms around me and sobbed. I hugged her back. "She's fine, honey. Have you called home?"

Jackie's body shook. "My baby. She's not my baby anymore."

"Yes, she's still your baby." I reassured her.

Charles walked up. "I hate to interrupt this sob-fest, but what the hell is going on?"

I broke away from Jackie. "Asshole."

"Yes, I'm an asshole, that's been long established, but this crying jag isn't going to help us catch this creep." Charles walked off toward William's house. "I'm going to check things out."

I called after him, "Hey, wait up." To Jackie I said, "Stay right here."

She wiped her eyes and nodded.

I ran after Charles, who didn't wait for me. Think it was because of that asshole remark? When I caught up to him, he was opening the gate to the backyard. I followed him. In for a dime, in for a dollar.

We walked around to the sliding glass door. Charles stopped up short.

"This curtain was wide open when I was back here before. Someone has been home."

"Check the door," I said. But being impatient, I checked it myself. Locked.

"Give me a minute." Charles pulled out his phone and walked away.

I did my best to listen in, but Charles had his back to me. I walked up behind him just as he was dialing a number. "What's going on?"

"I had my friend researching William. I called him to see if he found out where he worked." Charles put the phone to his ear and stopped talking.

"Where does he work?"

Before Charles could answer me, someone on the other line picked up. "Hi, may I speak with William Garrison?"

I waited while he listened. He tapped his phone and put it back in his pocket. "William left work early today. They asked if I wanted his voicemail."

"Give me a sec. Stay put." I ran back to my car and pulled out my lock picks. I was getting into this house, I didn't care what laws I was breaking. When I got back, I knelt down on my knees and started fiddling with the picks. This was a two-handed operation, and I was concentrating hard because I was a bit rusty.

"This is breaking and entering, Mimi." Charles stood over me like my protector.

"Not if I don't get caught." I kept at it until I heard a click. I had to turn hard because a sliding glass door had a different kind of lock, one that flipped over like a hook. "And we're in."

"Stay out here. I'm going in, not you. I'll take the rap on this." Charles helped me to my feet.

"Oh, no, it was my picking skills that got us this far. Either we go together, or you stay out here." I pulled the door open and stepped inside.

I looked back to see what Charles's decision was, and I saw him looking around. A second later, he was inside the Garrison house with me. Oh, what fun this was going to be. I loved snooping. I just hoped our snooping uncovered something we could use. Mostly, I hoped we didn't see Catey here.

Charles tapped me on the shoulder. I spun around, expecting something bad. He whispered, "Let's look around out here, then make our way down the hallway. Very quietly."

Right, like he needed to tell me to be quiet.

I looked at the room in front of us. The interior looked just like I expected, a tract home layout. We had entered a family room, with tan shag carpet and what looked like a hide-a-bed couch, just a shade darker than the carpet. There was a flat screen TV on the wall of dark paneling, the TV being the only thing updating this room from the 1970s.

Straight ahead was the counter Charles had mentioned earlier that day, but there was no backpack on it. The counter separated the family room from the kitchen, which was neat and tidy,no dishes in the sink, and the dishtowels folded next to the stove. Not so much as a magnet or picture on the refrigerator. How long had this guy lived here?

There was a set of double doors that were wide open and led to the living room. This room had more formal furniture. There was a matching three-piece set of a sofa, love seat and a club chair all centered around a burl wood coffee table. The pictures on the wall were seascapes, originals from what I could see. A stone fireplace graced the wall facing the backyard, a small basket of firewood sat on the floor next to it, and there were pictures in frames on the mantel. This is when Charles' reminder to be quiet came in handy. He must have seen the pictures at the same time I did. He put his hand over my mouth just as I inhaled deep and loud.

"Oh, shit," I said quietly under his fingers.

He turned me around to face him before removing his hands. He put a finger to his lips.

I looked back to the mantel and pointed. Charles looked, too. The framed pictures on the mantel were of Catey with her best friend, Anna. In another photo, Anna was standing with a younger girl, and William sat on a picnic table between them. This photo looked to be a few years older than the one with Catey and Anna. I had to turn away.

Charles pointed down the hall, and I let him lead this time. We stopped at the first door, which was open, and saw a small bedroom. It was sparsely furnished with a bed and dresser. There was a lamp on top of the dresser, but nothing personal in the room. I didn't bother to walk in and look in the closet. We moved on down the hall.

The second bedroom looked much like the first, only it seemed brighter. I'm not sure if it was the curtains, the walls, or the position of the room, but it seemed happier. I know it sounds weird, but the room did seem to have a better aura.

At the end of the hall was a bathroom. The orange wallpaper on the walls and the cream linoleum were dead giveaways as to the last time this room was redecorated. Everything in this house screamed rental, and this was the only room not model home tidy.

The toilet seat was up, and there seemed to be brownish red fluid speckling the bowl. The towels had been pulled from the rack, and were strewn on the floor. I saw this as the first sign something was amiss. I know, brilliant deduction.

Charles stepped in front of me and held me back by putting his hand up. I wanted to push into him, and even past him, heading for what I was sure was the master bedroom. I tempered myself and stayed behind him. I even stepped back as Charles pushed the bedroom door open.

He stepped into the room, and since I didn't hear him gasp, or the voices of anyone else, I followed him into the room. This room looked worse than the bathroom. The paisley bed cover was on the floor, and the white sheets were askew. I only saw one pillow on the bed, but assumed there were more on the floor. Usually a king size bed has more than one small pillow.

From my vantage point by the door, the bed was centered on the wall to my left, and there was an antique dresser directly in front of me. The top of the dresser was empty, but that was because the contents had been strewn across the floor. The drapes on the window were closed, but they were sheer, so plenty of light entered the space. I thought I saw movement, but it had to be my imagination because only Charles and I were in the room. I saw movement again, and realized it was birds flying in the backyard, fully visible through the sheers. When I looked down at the floor, I also saw men's shoes and a pair of pants on the far side of the bed.

When Charles walked to the far side of the room, I decided to follow, but I was looking at the items on the floor and slammed into him when he abruptly stopped.

Charles turned to me. "Get out of here now."

I looked past Charles to the shoes and pants on the floor. They appeared to be lying at a weird angle for being tossed on the carpet, but I didn't see anything to make Charles send me away.

"Why?" I couldn't just do what Charles said.

"Don't argue with me for once. Leave now. Please, Mimi, leave now!" Charles was no longer speaking in low tones, he was shouting at me.

Taken back, I did exactly the opposite of what he asked. I stepped around him toward the far side of the bed. In that very moment I wished, for once in my life, I'd taken orders without question. As I bolted from the room, I saw Charles dialing a number on his cell phone.

CHAPTER 5

I swear I barely made it to the front door before the police arrived. I went back to where Charles had parked to tell Jackie to go home. It was a needless trek as Jackie had already left. I know it shouldn't have, but her leaving made me suspicious.

When the police arrived and entered William Garrison's residence, Charles exited. I walked back to see why he stood in the yard instead of coming back to his car. Personally, I wanted to be as far from this house as I could get.

"Let's go," I said.

"Don't think so." Charles looked down the street. "Be warned, the homicide unit is on the way."

"Great." The homicide unit could possibly be Nick Christianson. I hoped it was anyone but him. Okay, in truth, I wanted to see him, as it'd been months since we last talked, but I didn't want to see him at a crime scene.

"Maybe you'll get lucky, and Nick will be the detective in charge." Charles gave me a little nudge.

"Or not."

There were at least half a dozen cops in the homicide unit, so the chances of it being Nick shouldn't be an issue. But those chances diminished to zilch as I saw the plain cop car skid to a stop in front of the

Garrison house. I turned my back to the street and stared at the house.

About this time, the neighbors came out of their houses to gawk. The neighbor to the right of the Garrison house walked up to me.

"What's going on?" He was an older man, I'd guess in his fifties, but still quite handsome. He wasn't much taller than my 5'7", but he seemed to tower over me. Maybe it was his build. It looked like his second job might be working out at the gym, and I liked the way his biceps bulged against the fabric of his polo shirt.

"Probably not my place to say." I didn't know this guy, so I didn't want to say anything I shouldn't.

"Well, something is going on. And since this is my next door neighbor, I think I should know."

Charles said, "There was a death."

"A death?" The neighbor sounded surprised, but seemed more curious.

"I probably shouldn't say anything more." Charles walked off and left me.

I thought about William's body on the floor next to the bed. Okay, I'm going to assume it was William, because the head was so bashed in the face wasn't recognizable. It may have had some identifiable features to someone who knew him. And to someone who knew the man very personally, his privates were exposed for identification. William still wore his socks, but his pants and boxer shorts were mere inches from his body.

As more neighbors gathered around the handsome guy, I headed toward the driveway, and them there to speculate.

I thought about the last time Nick and I met at a crime scene. In that case, the victim was very recognizable. It's just that her head was no longer attached to her body. I finally got the courage to turn and face the detectives as they approached.

Charles strode up to Nick and put his hand out. "Nick, wow, so good to see you. It's been a long time."

Nick, at a loss, shook Charles's hand. "It has been awhile." Then he looked at me, and back to Charles. "Why are you at my crime scene?"

Still jovial, Charles said, "Well, about that. You see, Mimi and I were here to visit with Mr. Garrison. Only when we arrived, Mr. Garrison wasn't in a position to accept visitors."

Nick aimed his next question at me. "So if he wasn't in a position to accept visitors, how is it you were in his house and found him dead on the floor in his bedroom?"

I looked at Charles, expecting him to give a calculated answer. Imagine my dismay when he just looked back at me like, "Well?"

Oh sure, when I want Charles to talk he doesn't, but get in a tight spot, he leaves it up to me. I hadn't planned on admitting we were in the house unless specifically asked. "We were looking for Jackie's daughter." The truth is always best in these situations, and this was a close to the truth as I could figure.

"Jackie? Would this be your friend and employee, Jackie?"

I nodded. The less said, the better.

The next question he addressed to Charles. "What would Jackie's daughter be doing at this house, and why would you assume she was here?"

Charles looked at me, but I just looked back at him and smiled. "It's really a very long story, and I'd love to tell you the whole thing, but maybe you want to get a look at the body before you ask us more questions," he said.

Nick's eyes went wide. "Charles, you're very lucky I like you. I usually don't take well to being told how to do my job."

All innocence, Charles said, "No, I'm not telling you how to do your job. It's just that this is a very long story, and there is more to it than a dead body. I could go into it in detail for you now if you like."

Nick shook his head. "You two stay put. I'll be back out here in a bit. Then you can bore me with all the details."

"I'd just like to say one thing," Charles called after Nick as he walked away.

Nick turned.

"You'll want to be sure you take his computer and cell phone into evidence," I said before Charles could speak.

Charles nodded, "What she said."

Nick continued into the house. That was when I noticed his partner as she stepped out from the passenger side of his Crown Vic.

"Now, that is one tall drink of water." Charles watched her walk toward the house.

"So cliché," I said. But he was right. She was as tall as Nick, if not taller. She wore a black pencil skirt that grazed the skin above her knees, and a black polo shirt with the Salinas Police Department logo. The skin that her uniform exposed was tight, tan, and covered well-defined muscles. This girl was an athlete. I immediately hated her.

She walked past us and smiled, but didn't speak.

We both turned and watched her walk into the house. She looked as good, if not better, from the back.

Her long blonde hair was pulled into a neat little bun at the nape of her neck.

I finally came to my senses and asked Charles, "I forgot to look at her face. Is she cute?"

"No, cute isn't a word I'd use to describe her." Charles still stared.

I was immediately relieved. No one should have a body like that and be cute, too.

Charles added, "She's freaking gorgeous."

There went the relief. I hated her more now. I didn't care if she was the nicest person on Earth. She was sexy as hell, and she was Nick's partner. Not that I wanted Nick, but I didn't want him to be partnered with *that*. But now it was all the more clear why we hadn't stayed in touch since Esme Bailey's murder was solved. I felt a little sick.

"Can we go?" I didn't want to be here when Nick and his partner came out of the house.

"Oh, Mimi, she's not after Nick. Suck it up and wait until they come back out. Besides, Nick told us to stay put."

"She could be engaged to Nick, and it wouldn't be any of my business. I don't care if she's a knock out." Lie, lie, lie. "I just hope she's a good partner for him, and they work well together."

Charles walked to the curb laughing out loud.

I followed after him. "What?"

"What a crock of crap. You have it so bad for that boy, you probably have a vibrator named Nick."

I nearly choked. But I was afraid to say anything. If I told him I didn't have a vibrator, he'd say I needed to get one. If I said I didn't name my vibrators, he'd say I should. There was no good response.

Charles panted and fanned himself. "Nick, oh, Nick."

He sat on the curb just as he said it, and his head was in prime position for me to smack it, so I did.

"Ouch." He rubbed his head and laughed. "Just invite him to your house, seduce him, and be done with it."

I sat beside him. I didn't want to seduce anyone; I wanted to be seduced. "I'm going to have lunch with Sebastian."

This time Charles nearly choked. "Huh? You can't be serious."

"I am serious. He said he's been trying to work up the courage to ask me out for months. He didn't want me to think he was such a creep."

"He's not a creep, but he's certainly not your type." Charles pushed up his sleeves to make a point.

"But something tells me the sex would be so hot. I'm thinking just a one-night stand." I couldn't really see myself in bed with Sebastian, but it was fun to get a reaction out of Charles.

"Mimi, you wouldn't know what a one-night stand was if you sat on it. Sebastian may be mysterious, but remember, you are having sex with everyone he ever had sex with. Let's see, that would include not only a murder victim who literally lost her head, but would also include a murderer. Think about that while you are in the throes of passion."

"Yup, Charles, once again you've ruined it for me. I just wanted a night of being someone other than me for a change, and you tainted it."

"If you want a night of being someone else, join a LARP. Don't have sex with someone you'd never even consider." Charles's words sounded light, but his face was dead serious.

LARP, live action role-playing, was exactly what Sebastian did in his spare time. Not all of his spare time, but he and a few others ran a vampire game played in Santa Cruz.

Resigned, I said, "I know. It's not like I'd ever do anything with Sebastian. I can fantasize all I want about being a bad girl, but it's just not me. Though I would love to have sex with him, and make sure Susan knew about it."

"You want to lose your head, too?" Charles reminded me of her modus operandi.

Susan was psycho, but for the time being, she was behind bars. Somehow, even though she already tried to kill me once, I wanted to flaunt a relationship with her ex-boyfriend. I'd give her a reason to want to kill me this time.

That sounded vindictive, and I'm not that kind of person. But it's hard not to want to do bad things to someone who wanted me dead.

Before I could answer Charles, we heard a commotion behind us. I looked to see "hot and gorgeous" dashing from the house and out to the street. She barely reached the curb before she spewed liquid and chunks like a fire hose. I had to turn away.

Charles jumped up and pulled off his shirt. She stood with her knees slightly bent, her hands resting on them, and didn't even look up as Charles offered his shirt for her to wipe her mouth.

I stared in complete shock. I'd never seen Charles be even remotely chivalrous, not even to another man. What did this woman have that I didn't? What did she have that other women didn't? When I'd puked at Nick's murder scene a few months back, he was livid. He wasn't even following his partner out of the house to reprimand her.

Correct that. Nick charged out the door. He looked incensed and made a beeline straight for his partner. I tensed, waiting for the barrage of harsh words.

He stopped next to her and put his hand on her upper back. "You okay?"

What? I jumped up, furious. Before I could stop myself, I stomped over to the puking woman. "I puke at your crime scene, and you all but cuss me out. She's a detective who should know better, and you baby her? What the hell is wrong with this picture?"

What the hell was wrong with me? I'm not a jealous person, but I could feel a rage bubbling inside me, and I was pretty sure it had nothing to do with vomit. But I didn't back down.

Nick glowered at me, then grabbed my arm and escorted me to the driver's side of his car.

I went willingly, not sure if I was pissed off, or beyond embarrassed.

"What the hell is wrong with you? Are you a nut job?"

"Excuse me?" I decided I was pissed.

"She's a cop. She belongs at that crime scene, and this is her first murder. She's entitled to get a little sick when the victim's head is bashed in like a ripe pumpkin."

I yanked my arm away from him. "Well, I'd say a decapitation is worse than that creepy assed pedophile lying on the floor in his bedroom with his pants down. Too bad his dick wasn't cut off, too."

Nick started to berate me again, and then said, "Pedophile? Oh, no, Mimi, what's going on?"

I leaned against Nick's car and told him the whole story about Jackie's daughter, the text messages, and everything I knew, which wasn't much at this point.

"Is that why you were in his house? You were actually looking for Jackie's daughter?"

"Jackie went to give Catey back the cell phone she confiscated, but Catey wasn't in school. Charles didn't want to delete the text messages because we didn't want her to know we were able to get into her phone. William had sent Catey a message with his address." I took a deep breath. "Jackie saw the message, and when Catey wasn't at the school, she came here looking for her."

"Where is Jackie now?" Nick's face burned with fury.

I cringed. "I don't know."

"You. Don't. Know." Nick spat the words. "You realize Jackie may be our murderer, right? Why is it that you don't think straight when your friends are involved in bad shit?"

"Jackie didn't kill William. She was never even in the house." So there, you pompous jerk. "She was still in the truck when we arrived, just staring at the house."

"I'm not done with you yet. I'm going back over to talk to Piper and see if she's okay. I want you to bring Jackie to the police station ASAP." Nick walked back to Charles and Piper.

Charles asked her, "You going to be okay?"

Piper had stopped retching, but she still looked pale. "I'm so embarrassed."

I looked around, and noticed that even more neighbors had gathered. The man who was talking to me earlier was animated and gesturing. He had a group of housewives gathered around him.

Another patrol car arrived, and when the officer got out of the car, Nick said, "Get crime scene tape up around the perimeter of the property, stat."

The officer popped the trunk and grabbed the yellow tape.

When the other uniformed officer walked over, Nick said, "Start canvassing the neighborhood, ask them if they saw or heard anything. Let's get moving on this."

I looked around and saw another neighbor, a woman of about fifty, standing on her porch. She didn't try to come over to the yard, or get closer; she just stood there. Across the street, a man in his sixties retreated back into the house as soon as he saw the officer approaching him. Several other neighbors stood on the sidewalk and the street.

Piper seemed to be doing better and handed Charles back his shirt. Charles said, "No, no, you keep it. I have plenty more."

Nick approached. "Detective Mason, you ready to go back inside, or would you like to stay out here a bit longer?"

Detective Piper Mason. I hated her on site. She was stunning, and vulnerable, and the boys just couldn't get enough. Funny, Nick had called her Piper when talking to me, but Detective Mason in front of Charles. I'd just bet that they were sleeping together. No, no, I wasn't going to think like that, it wasn't my business. I walked back to the trio.

"Detective Mason, I'm sorry for my outburst. I had a similar incident a few months back, and Detective Christianson wasn't nearly as respectful. You are lucky he likes having you as a partner." I started to put my hand out to shake, but thought better of it. "By the way, I'm Mimi Capurro. I own the Gotcha Detective Agency."

"Hi Ms. Capurro, I wish we could have met on better terms. I've heard a lot about you."

Well, if that didn't take my breath away. I covered by stammering, "This, uh, this is my associate, the shirtless wonder, Charles Parks."

Charles performed a slight bow, nicely contracting his abdominals. "Nice to meet you, Detective Mason. I always enjoy a memorable introduction. Rest assured, I'll always remember this one."

Piper laughed. She seemed to be getting her color back.

"I'd love to stick around for this cocktail party, but I have a dead body in the house," Nick said, as he left us standing at the curb. When he reached the front door, he turned back and said, "I'll be here until the crime scene techs finish processing the scene. Mimi, I want to see you, Charles and Jackie in my office in two hours. Got it?"

Charles cooed, "He wants to see you."

I snapped back. "He wants to see *us*."

Nick disappeared into the house. Piper headed to Nick's car and sat in the passenger seat.

Charles called to her, "Nice meeting you. See you around."

I nudged him. "What the hell?"

We started to our car before Charles responded. "I take care of my kind."

I looked back at the detective, who had her head in her hands. "Your kind?"

"Oh, yeah, I know Detective Mason and I will be fast friends."

Charles opened the passenger door for me, went around to the driver's side and got in. He put his Spyder in gear and laid rubber, showing off for his new detective friend.

"I just know Nick is screwing her."

Charles roared with laughter. "Oh, God, now that's a good one."

CHAPTER 6

I was out of options, and we had to be at the police station in 15 minutes. I'd tried Jackie's house, the YMCA where she took kickboxing, her salon (though who'd go to the salon with this mess at hand?), and even back to Catey and Corey's school. At a dead end, I did what I always do: I went to Charles.

Since Gemma had the afternoon off, Charles was manning the reception area. I saw him fiddling with his phone, which he promptly put away when he saw me.

"What are you doing?" I asked casually, not wanting him to think I was being nosey.

"Nothing."

Way too abrupt an answer for him, so I knew he was up to something. "No, really, what are you doing?"

Charles got his phone back out. He showed me the screen. "I'm tracking Jackie."

"What?" I was amazed and thrilled at the same time. Then I thought about it. "Wait a minute, something about this is a bit disturbing."

He sat the phone on the reception desk. "All of the work phones have GPS chips embedded in them. Jackie happens to have her work phone with her."

"All of the phones?"

"Yes, Mimi, even yours. I thought it was the best way to be sure of your safety while out in the field. If you don't answer for some reason, like Jackie isn't answering now, I can at least know where you are."

This was Charles at his brilliant best. He thought of the techie things that made us a better and safer business. I can't tell you how many angry spouses I've dealt with over the last few years. The women are far worse than the men. I can run at a good clip, I carry a stun gun and, a pistol, and I pack a good punch, but some of the women still scare me.

Just to play devil's advocate, I said, "What if we're separated from our phone?"

"Hasn't happened yet, but I'll probably get you drunk some night and embed a chip in your ass. Then you'll never lose your ass for anything." He laughed.

I grabbed the phone from Charles. "Come on, we have less than fifteen minutes to find Jackie, snatch her up, and get to the cop shop before Nick puts out an APB."

Charles dashed past me. "I'm driving."

Fine. Driving with Charles in the passenger seat was like being in driver's ed all over again. I got in the passenger seat of my Land Rover and let Charles play sleuth as we tracked Jackie down. I kept watching to screen on Charles' phone to make sure the blip didn't move to another location.

I'd tried to track Jackie at all of her favorite haunts, but I should have been looking for Catey's favorite places. She was sitting with Catey, sharing a messy looking sundae at Baskin Robbins. Watching them stuff ice cream in their mouths made me wish we didn't have to interrupt. It also made me realize I hadn't eaten since this morning.

Charles parked right in front of the ice cream shop and waited. "Well?"

"Well what?" I knew he wanted me to go in and get Jackie.

"I've already been the bad guy enough today. You go in there and tear her away from her daughter."

I moved as if I had cement blocks strapped to my ankles. I did not want to go in there. Before I could even drag my butt from the car, Jackie was out the door and jogging toward me.

My voice went really low. "Don't you ever take off like that, and not answer calls or texts ever again. If you do, I don't need you working for me."

Jackie stopped dead in her tracks. "You don't need me as it is. I'm the one who needs you."

This broke my heart, and I mentally kicked myself for being harsh. "I'm serious. I've been scared to death. I was so worried about you."

"I'm sorry, but I found Catey back at the school. She said she was in the nurse's office when I was there earlier. I gave her back her phone, and now here we are. We've been talking everything out. Oh, I have so much to tell you." Jackie looked ten years younger than she did this morning.

"It's going to have to wait. We have to be in Nick's office," I looked at my watch, "about five minutes ago."

"The police station? Why?" I swear Jackie twitched.

"He knows you were there earlier today. He wants to talk to all of us."

"Nick is a homicide detective. What could he possibly want to talk with us about?"

Only then did I realize Jackie didn't know that Charles and I found William's body in the bedroom. I didn't say anything about it in the dozen or so voice messages I left her. I didn't want to spook her. "Jackie, I don't know how to tell you this, but William Garrison is dead."

I said this just as Catey walked up to the car. Her eyes were a bit swollen, and she avoided looking at me. "Mom, I'm going to walk home."

"No, I'll give you a ride, honey. Give me just a minute." Jackie tossed her car keys to Catey, but she didn't catch them.

"Hey, Catey." It wasn't like her not to acknowledge me, and I was a bit put off.

"Hey, Mimi." She still wouldn't look at me.

She bent down and picked up the keys. Handing them back to her mom, she said, "I really need to walk this ice cream off. I'll see you at the house."

Jackie said, "Well, wasn't that perfect timing? Shit."

Charles leaned over from the driver's seat. "We found William dead in his bedroom. His head was bashed in. Now get in the damn car before we have warrants out for our arrests."

So much for Charles not wanting to be the bad guy.

"I'll follow you in my car." Jackie started to walk away.

Charles jumped out of the car and cut Jackie off. He gently took her by the elbow and steered her to the back door on the driver's side. "Get in. I'm not going to track you all over Salinas again today. We'll bring you back to your car later."

Jackie didn't protest. She climbed into the backseat as I got back in the passenger side. Charles had the car rolling before we had the doors closed.

Just as Charles maneuvered the Land Rover into a parallel parking space on Lincoln Street, my phone rang. I looked at the caller I.D., and saw it was Nick. "Oh, no."

"What?" Charles and Jackie said in unison.

"It's Nick," I answered. "I haven't seen this number on my phone in a long time."

"Where the hell are you? You were supposed to be here half an hour ago."

"Oh, well, nice to talk to you, too. We're out in front of the police station, just getting out of the car, as a matter of fact." And I was. I stepped out of the car and jaywalked across the street. Charles and Jackie trailed after me, close on my heels.

"I do have other business. It would've been nice of you to show up on time." Nick hung up.

We walked into the police reception where I expected we'd have to tell the officer at the desk we were here to see Detective Christianson, but alas, Detective Mason was there to greet us.

"Hello again." Charles and Piper did a double kiss on each cheek as if they were old buddies. Barf.

Charles shoved Jackie forward. "This is Jackie Baccarin, she's a friend of ours. Detective Christianson is expecting us."

Piper smiled and led us back to the inner workings of the cop shop.

I leaned in close to Piper. "Is he in a bad mood?"

She looked over her shoulder. "Who, Nick? I'm not sure Nick knows what a bad mood is."

I knew it; they were doing it. She was completely blindsided by having sex with him. Not that I cared, but I would feel bad for her when he dumped her and moved on. Nick never did stay in a relationship long.

I felt a vibration, then my phone rang, "*Hello, it's your mother calling.*" I answered quickly, thinking I needed to change that ringtone.

"Hi, Mom, I can't talk right now. I'm at the police station." This was going to go over well.

"The police station?" The alarm in her voice was audible.

I knew this was going to happen. Why did I tell her I was here? "I'm visiting with Nick."

"Oh, tell Nick hi for me." A beat, then she said, "I thought you were through with him."

"There's nothing to be through with." We'd reached Nick's desk. "I gotta go. I'll call you later."

"Tell him hi." She disconnected.

Nick stood when he saw us. "Let's go to a conference room. It's a little cramped in here."

We all turned right back around and left the homicide department for the main police room. Nick led the way to a conference room across the hall.

I watched him walking away, remembering what it was like to spend time with him. Riding in his Boxter, laughing... *Oh, stop, just stop it.* But seeing him in those slacks with the V-neck cashmere sweater, I wanted to get my hands on him just one more time. *Really, this had to stop.*

Piper said, "Can I get anyone any coffee, water, soda?"

Charles said, "No thanks." Jackie and I shook our heads.

"Nick, anything?" She drooled.

He ignored her and pulled out a chair for Jackie and me. Piper left the room.

"Let's get started. We're already way behind. But on a positive note, I have more information than I had thirty minutes ago."

Nick sat on the other side of the table. Charles stood by the door.

"So what do you need from us?" I said.

Nick looked at Charles. "Can you please lock the door?"

Charles looked at the door, then Nick, then the door. "But, Det-- I mean Piper is…"

"Please lock the door," Nick said, more firmly.

Charles locked it.

"Here's the deal," Nick started, then stopped and looked pointedly at Jackie. "You were in that house."

Jackie started to protest, but Nick held up his hand.

Charles looked at her. "Jackie?"

"Don't say anything, Jackie. I'm not recording, but when Piper gets back in here, we will be." Nick looked at me. "This is a favor I'm doing for you."

"Me?" I was shocked. I hadn't heard from the man in months, and now he's doing me some sort of favor?

To Jackie, he said, "Your fingerprints are all over that damn house. Don't even try to tell me you weren't in there."

I looked at Jackie. "You lied to me?"

Charles got right in her face. "You fucking lied to me?"

Jackie just stared forward. She didn't deny anything. She didn't speak.

I turned my chair toward her. "What the hell is going on? Jackie, tell me what's going on."

Jackie sat calmly. "I plead the fifth."

Charles slammed his hand on the conference table. "The fifth? No, you don't."

I stood. "Charles, calm down. Getting upset isn't going to help things."

This was bad. First, Charles never lost his temper. Second, he hated being lied to. Third, I was caught in the middle.

He turned on me. "Calm down? Calm down? We broke into a house where there was a dead man, and you want me to calm down?" Charles paced. "And you, Jackie, you knew there was a dead guy in that damned house, and you let us break in. Calm down?"

Now he was repeating himself, another thing he didn't do. This was really bad.

"Charles, did I hear you say you broke into William Garrison's house?"

Oh, no. I wanted to crawl under that table and dig a hole to China.

Suddenly Charles calmed considerably. "Excuse me?"

"Never mind. When Piper gets back in here, I'm going to have to arrest you, Jackie."

Jackie's eyes went wide. "What?"

"There was no reason for your fingerprints to be in that house, and they were everywhere: the kitchen, the living room, and the picture frame of your daughter with William's daughter. What were you doing in that house?"

I stepped in before Jackie replied. "Were her prints on the murder weapon?"

Nick said, "There was no murder weapon. Whoever did this took it with them."

I looked at Jackie. She stared at the wall. Charles stared at her. Nick stared at all of us. This interview, and this day, weren't going as I'd planned.

"If Catey was friends with William's daughter, Anna, there's reason for Jackie's prints to be in the house. Maybe she'd picked up Catey from the house before." Charles sounded like a lawyer.

"Plausible," Nick said. "Jackie, did you know William Garrison was Anna's dad?"

Jackie finally came to. "Let me tell you something, Nick. If that son of a bitch hadn't been dead with I walked in that house, I would have killed him myself." She stood. "Arrest me, because whoever killed that low life scum should be given an award. I'd gladly go to prison to be sure that man would never prowl after another young girl."

"Okay, Jackie, you've said enough." I was getting scared. I didn't want to see my friend go to prison.

"Did you look at his laptop? It was out there in the open. And guess what? Right before I arrived at his house, he sent my daughter," Jackie's eyes welled and her voice cracked, "my precious fourteen-year-old daughter, a picture of his penis. So understand this, if I'd have killed him, I'd have tied him up and clipped his penis off, one snip at a time with toenail clippers. Then I'd have left him there to bleed out as I cut off his balls."

Both Nick and Charles's hands involuntarily moved to their crotches. I even felt a bit of a cringe.

Nick walked across the room and unlocked the door. Piper walked in, but she didn't have any of the amenities she'd gone out for. She walked up to Jackie and said, "You are under arrest for the murder of William Garrison…" She put her hand on Jackie's arm and walked her out the door.

I could see Jackie tense in Piper's hand as they walked away. Then she turned, "What about my kids?"

"I've got it, honey," I said. "I'll pick them up, and they can stay with me tonight."

Charles stopped Piper before she was out the door. "Jackie, I'm on top of things. We'll get this straightened out, I promise. And I don't make promises to anyone, you know that."

Jackie kissed Charles on the cheek, and the two women walked away.

"And don't ever lie to me again." Charles admonished, and then turned on Nick. "You really are an asshole, aren't you?"

"Watch it, Charles. I'm still a cop."

"So fucking arrest me for calling you an asshole, and you'll have two innocent people in your jail cells tonight." Charles spun on his heel to leave.

"And don't get involved in this case either, Charles," Nick yelled after him.

Charles turned back and stalked toward Nick. Standing right in his face, he said, "I could give a shit if you find the killer. That pervert deserved to die. But I do care that you are booking my friend, an innocent person, on murder charges. So the only thing I'll be doing is trying to prove her innocence." Then Charles pointed in Nick's face. "And you'd better not get in *my* way."

I couldn't believe my eyes. Nick backed up a step. I thought for sure he was going to punch Charles in the face. Instead he turned and looked at me.

"I can hold her for forty-eight hours without filing any charges. Got it? You have forty-eight hours. Understand, this isn't about being friends. If she's guilty, I'll put her ass away for life."

Charles backed down a bit. "Deal. But you'd better make her comfortable while she's here."

Nick just walked past Charles without acknowledging him. He didn't even look at me as he left the room.

I just whispered, "Forty-eight hours."

CHAPTER 7

When I arrived at Jackie's house, both Corey and Catey were home. Corey was playing X-Box in the living room, and Catey was sitting at the kitchen table doing what looked like math homework. I really hope I wasn't expected to help with the homework, since it all looked like foreign scribbles to me.

I knew they weren't identical twins (opposite sex and all), but they looked so much alike. And as much as I hate their father, I'm so glad they didn't get Jackie's red hair. Both were more of a strawberry blonde. They did, however, inherit her pale skin. Corey embraced his good looks: strawberry-blonde, pale skin, and light blue eyes. Catey, on the other hand, had saved money to have her hair highlighted, and could tell the experts how to make a spray tan look real.

"Where's Mom?" Corey stopped killing people on his game long enough to grant me some attention when I walked in.

"Come sit with me and Catey in the kitchen," I said. I ran my fingers through my hair, not sure how I was going to explain.

Corey reluctantly stopped his game and followed me. He sat next to Catey and stared at me.

I sat across from them and lied. God help me I lied. "Your mom is working with the police tonight.

She's probably not going to be home until very late, so she wants you to stay with me."

In stereo, Corey and Catey moaned, "What?"

"What's she working on?" Corey asked.

I looked at Catey, who conveniently looked away. "There's a case she's involved with, and she's helping the police with some of the evidence."

"Cool. What kind of case?" Corey found this almost as interesting as his game.

Catey chimed in. "Corey, when will you ever learn? Mom and Mimi love to keep their secrets."

"Not secrets. It's called confidentiality. We can't reveal the details of cases we work." I was hoping this would quash any further questions.

"Whatever. It's not like we'd know who these people are anyway." Corey still looked disappointed that he wasn't going to get the goods.

"I think I'll just stay here," Catey said.

"Gee, thanks, nice to feel so loved," I said.

"It's not that," she explained. "It's just that we have all of our stuff here. And I have so much homework."

When I walked in, Catey didn't look like her mind was on her homework. She'd been staring off into space, but I didn't dare mention that now.

"Tell you what. Corey, you can bring your box thingy and play on my fifty-two inch flat screen." I paused as Corey's expression said it all. "And I'll order out for pizza, anything you want, and we can watch scary movies until it's time for school in the morning."

Corey jumped up. "Mom's going to be pissed! I'm so doing this."

Catey slammed her math book shut and started packing her things into her backpack. "It looks like there's no way out of this, so I want garden vegetarian pizza."

God, I was going to suck at being a parent. I just lied, and then bribed these kids. "Fine."

Corey jumped up and went into the living room to disassemble his gaming gadget so he could bring it to my house.

"I'm ready," Catey said, as she slung her backpack over her shoulder.

"Catey, honey, toothbrush, clean underwear?"

"Oh, yeah." She shuffled at a snail's pace toward her bedroom.

* * *

It was dark by the time we arrived back at my house. I reached for my driver's door to get out of the car, and a hand came from nowhere and opened the door for me. I jumped and screamed.

"Holy shit." Now, I'd like to say I'm not normally the jumpy type, but I am.

"Hey."

"Seriously, are you trying to kill me?" I said.

"Not really."

The twins snickered.

I tossed my keys to Corey. "Go in the house. I'll be in in a bit. And let Lola out to pee, please."

"No way, she won't come back in the house for me," Corey said.

A little impatient, I said, "Then just leave her out."

The kids ran to the house, and I got out of my car, but left the door ajar. "What do you want?"

"I don't want you to be mad at me for doing my job." Nick stood solemn, and I could see his grey eyes shining from the interior light of my Land Rover.

"It's hard not to hate you right now." I couldn't lie about that.

"Come on, Mimi, it's my job. I'm a homicide detective, remember? Unlike you, I don't get to pick and choose my cases. And this one is my case."

"Well, you and Piper have a good time detecting then." I tried to move past him.

"Piper Mason is a good detective."

"When she's not puking all over your crime scene." *Oh, that was mature, Mimi, so mature.*

"I just came to tell you that I'm looking at all other avenues. I don't think Jackie is guilty either, but Piper thinks there's enough evidence to convict her. All we needed was the murder weapon."

"Well, go find it."

Nick looked down, before looking me in the eye. "We already did."

I took a deep breath. Oh, the relief. "So Jackie is on her way home?"

"We found it in the back of your Toyota pickup, Mimi."

Remember the puking thing? Well, the bile was working its way into a frothy bubble with those words. I tried to respond, but I couldn't.

"That's not even funny, Nick." I pushed him away and started toward the house.

Nick grabbed me by the arm. "Have you ever heard of obstruction of justice?"

"What the hell are you talking about?"

"The murder weapon was in the back of the truck Jackie was driving. You said you saw her in it, didn't you?"

I thought back. I couldn't remember, but…"Yes, she was sitting in the Toyota when we arrived at William's house."

"And you didn't see the bloody baseball bat in the bed of the pickup?"

"I didn't look in the back of the pickup." I hesitated. "Nick, Jackie is a detective, too. She'd never be stupid enough to put the murder weapon in plain sight in my vehicle. This smacks of set up."

"And who would want to set Jackie up?"

"Well, someone…" I fought my head for an answer, "someone."

Nick nodded. "There're a lot of explanations. I'm going to get to the bottom of this, I promise. And when I do, I only hope that Jackie is just caught in the middle and not the culprit."

I felt my body slump. I was exhausted. My day had started with me feeling like a cougar, and now, I felt rode hard and put away wet. Overworked and unloved.

Nick stepped closer and wrapped his arms around me. I stiffened. It should have felt good to be held like that. I tried to hold out, but I gave in and hugged him back. I needed something solid in that moment. That cashmere sweater was as soft as I'd imagined, and the muscles felt harder than I remembered.

I don't think he had been holding me for more than a few seconds, when I heard someone call my name. I looked up to see a man dressed in plaid skater shorts and a pink polo shirt. He was tall, well built, and damn it, he was handsome, tattoos and all.

I broke away from Nick's embrace. "Hey, Sebastian. How are you?"

I was a little creeped out that he was at my house, but I would never let on to Nick. I walked over and stood on my tiptoes to kiss him on the lips. It was all I could do to keep from laughing when I saw the look on Nick's face. Well, he had Piper, and now I had Sebastian.

"Sorry I'm late. I was detained. Come on inside." Oh, this was fun.

I started toward the house with my hand on Sebastian's elbow. He played along very nicely, only giving me "the look" after we'd turned away from Nick.

"Thanks for checking on me, Nick. Sebastian will be here with me tonight, so no worries."

Nick stepped onto the curb. "Can I have just one more minute with you?"

I looked at Sebastian, and he nodded. "I'll be right back."

Sebastian waited on the porch as I walked back to the curb. He never even acknowledged Nick.

"What the hell is this?" Nick spat.

"What?" I loved playing dumb.

"Him." Nick was so rude as to actually point at Sebastian.

"What about him? He has nothing to do with your murder investigation." Oh, I was good. Or at least that's what I told myself.

"I can't believe it. You're dating a guy half your age. You must be really desperate." Nick walked away.

His words stung, but I wasn't going to let him see just how much. "Oh, believe me, he can service me better than any old fart my age can. Desperation has nothing to do with it." I laughed, but it even sounded fake to me.

He got in his car and sped way.

I stood there looking at his taillights, not even realizing that Sebastian had come up behind me. He put his strong hands on my shoulders. "Are you okay?"

I turned and buried my face in his chest. Crying, I said, "No, I'm not okay."

He held me, and kissed the top of my head. And I think at that moment, I realized that he was truly a nice guy.

"Come on, let's go in the house, and you can tell me what's going on." He walked me to the house.

But when we got to the porch, I realized I couldn't talk to him about anything. The twins were in the house. I wiped my tears, and put on my game face.

"Before we go in, I think you should know, the twins are staying with me tonight."

His face was blank for a moment, before he said, "I'd love to meet the twins. How old are they?"

I didn't have to answer the question. Corey opened the door and yelled, "I can't get it to work."

I turned. "Get what to work?"

"My game. Your TV is way different from ours. And you promised."

I looked at Sebastian. "Meet Corey."

"Cool tats, man."

"Thanks." Sebastian looked at me and smiled, then back to Corey. "Let me see if I can help with your game."

Catey sat on the couch, texting on her phone. I walked over and took it from her.

"Hey!" She reached out to grab it back.

"This is my house, my rules. No texting when you can enjoy conversing with the people right here in the room." I tucked her phone in my pocket.

"Mimi!" Catey whined like a pro.

Sebastian said, "Your kids call you by your first name?"

Everyone looked at him wide-eyed, and the room went silent.

I laughed. "They aren't mine."

Corey and Catey said, in stereo, "Yuck, she's not our mom."

Now it was my turn to whine. "Yuck? Really, yuck?"

Corey spoke up, while Catey went back to moping. "You wouldn't be so cool as a mom. Kids need structure, you know."

Sebastian laughed. And that was that. Corey and Sebastian played the shooting game, and yelled at the screen. He even got Catey involved, teaching her how to shoot, and how the game worked. Catey was good.

When Sebastian invited me to play, I held up my glass of Argentinean Malbec. "I'm good."

"Oh, I'll take one of those." Sebastian let Catey take over his spot in the game and sat next to me on the couch. I just happened to have a second glass on the coffee table, so I poured.

He took the glass and held it up a bit, swirling and sniffing it. I nearly spit my wine out trying to keep from laughing. Then he took a sip.

"Intense fruity aroma. I'm going to say, raspberry, plum and maybe even a hint of blackberry on first sniff. Very nice for a light-bodied Malbec."

Now I really was laughing. Aloud. Uncontrollably.

"What?" Sebastian sat his glass on the table.

"I'm sorry. I just never would have imagined those words coming from your mouth." I'd regained my composure.

"How soon we forget. I thought I told you, Henry, Eugene and I love wine."

Ah, that's right. One of the pieces of evidence in Esme Bailey's murder investigation was a bottle of wine that had been drugged.

I looked up at the twins, who were oblivious to us as they terrorized each other while playing their game.

"It's a nice night. Let's take this bottle and go outside."

Lola was still in the yard. She sat on the grass in the far corner, next to her dog house. Her Doberman ears were on high alert, even though she looked ridiculous with the stuffed bear in her mouth. I gave the bear about two days before she buried it, which was longer than most of Lola's toys last before she killed them.

Sebastian squatted down. "What's her name?"

"Lola, but you don't want to engage her. She's not much for strangers."

He called her over anyway, and she trotted straight to him. He petted her between the ears, and she promptly dropped the bear at his feet. I was delighted. Lola never shared her toys with anyone but me. Maybe Sebastian was really a good guy, and I had good judgment for a change. But then again, she seemed to like Nick, too.

We sat on the wooden swing, still holding our glasses of wine. It was quiet as Sebastian threw Lola's bear across the yard, and she took off after it. There was no retrieving, as Lola knew that game, and *never* brought the toy back.

"Do you mind if I ask what's going on with you and Nick?" He wasn't looking at me when he asked. He stared off into the darkness.

"Nothing is going on with us." I looked over my shoulder to be sure the twins were out of earshot. "He stopped by to explain that he has my best friend locked up in his jail cell because it's his job."

"Ouch. What happened?" He looked at me now.

"It's a long story." I sighed.

"I have all night." He actually shifted his body to face me.

So I told him. About the cell phone, William (but I didn't say his name), the murder, the weapon, and Nick arresting Jackie. He listened, not once interrupting me. It felt good to talk it out.

"Wow, what a day. Are you okay?" He touched my leg.

My body reacted more violently than I'd planned. I wanted more. So I scooted a bit closer, turned my back, and leaned into him. He wrapped his arms around me and kissed the top of my head.

And I don't know how it happened, but somehow I'd turned my head and kissed him full on the lips. He kissed me back. I kissed him again.

He pulled me back away to arm's length and asked, "So that's what the hug was all about? Nothing more?"

Still lost in his dreamy kiss, I said, "What?"

"Nick was holding you pretty tight when I arrived. It was just a friendly hug?"

I sat back. "That's all it was."

"So then why did you act like you were expecting me?"

I thought for a minute. Lie? No, I didn't want to lie. "I wanted Nick to leave. And when you showed up out of nowhere, I thought if I acted like I was expecting you, Nick would feel unwelcome and leave. And he did."

"You never even asked me why I'm here." He took a long sip from his wineglass.

"I guess after I saw how great you are with the twins, I didn't care why you're here." I truly did forget that he'd arrived uninvited.

"I actually stopped by to apologize for bothering you at work. I should never have come by to discuss a private matter in your place of business." He took yet another long sip of wine.

I grabbed the bottle and started to refill his glass.

"No, I want to be sober when I tell you this. I want you to know I'm completely sincere."

Now I took a long sip of wine. I didn't want to be sober when I heard what he had to say.

"I won't bother you anymore. I just needed to get it off my chest that I can't stop thinking about you. The weird thing is that this isn't like me. I've never had any trouble getting a girl out of my head. But, seriously, I masturbate thinking of you."

Okay, then. "Sebastian--"

"Okay, that came out more crude than I'd planned. I'm not perfect. But what I'm really trying to say is that the next move is yours. I told you how I feel, I invaded your house tonight, and I just embarrassed you by being crude, so now I'm done." He started to stand.

I stopped him. "Sit." Then I said, "This is my next move." I kissed him again, and it felt as good as it had the first time.

Between kisses, Sebastian said, "Oh, Mimi, I want you so much."

And then I heard, "When are we ordering pizza?"

CHAPTER 8

Damn, damn, damn. I should never have polished off that bottle of wine with the pizza. I'm not twenty-five anymore, and even the extra water and ibuprofen before going to bed didn't help much. Everything sounded magnified, and I had teen twins in the backseat of my car. I was only too happy that they were ignoring me and had shoved their ear buds in their ears as soon as they buckled up.

Once at the school, I thought for sure they'd want me to park a block or two down, so no one saw their crazy "Aunt Mimi" dropping them off, but they let me drive right up to the front of the school.

Catey yelled before she was even out of the car, "Hey, Anna, wait up." I thought my head would explode.

I looked across the schoolyard to see Anna stop and look up at Catey. I asked, "Hey, Catey, who is that with Anna?"

"Her mom, why?" Catey hesitated just long enough to answer. But she was out the door before I could tell her why.

Anna's mom. I wondered just how much she knew. Then I saw a little girl run up to Anna's mom, wearing a *Hello Kitty* backpack.

"Later, Mimi. Thanks for the sleepover and the pizza." Corey slipped out a bit more quietly than Catey did.

I just wished it was Sebastian saying thanks. He made a hasty exit when the pizza arrived last night. I'm not sure why I kept drinking the wine after he left. Was it to rid myself of wanting him to stay? Or was I trying to forget kissing him? All I knew was the whole thing made me nauseous this morning.

Lola leaned across from the passenger seat and licked me in the face, which brought me out of my trance, and I drove to the agency.

* * *

Charles sat at the kitchen table when I walked in. He was bent over, adjusting his argyle socks. The socks just happened to bear the same shade of lavender as his polo shirt, and the navy of his slacks. I reached out and mussed his hair, just to piss him off.

"Not going to happen." Charles fingered his blonde locks back into place.

"What's not going to happen?" I reached for a coffee cup from the cupboard.

"You aren't going to rile me this morning. I don't have time for it." He stood, straightened his slacks and left the room.

This was not my normal Charles. I abandoned the coffee and caught up to him. "What's going on?"

"Maybe I should ask you that question," Charles grinned from ear to ear.

"Oh, no, what's going on?" Suddenly I felt a dread far worse than a hangover.

"Nick stopped by last night."

"He stopped by your place?" So his visit wasn't exclusive to me. My heart flipped at bit. I thought he was worried about me.

"He wanted to let me know that he's still looking for the killer, and that he doesn't think Jackie is the guilty party. But at the same time, she's looking like their best suspect right now."

"Yeah, he stopped by my house last night, too, and said the same thing." I still didn't understand why he felt the need to talk to Charles personally, too.

Charles started to walk away again, and then turned, "Oh, and he wanted to know how long you and Sebastian had been dating."

Yes! was what I was thinking, but I said, "Really? That's weird, don't you think? What would make him ask that?"

"Oh, I don't know, Mimi, maybe it was the way you were flaunting him in front of Nick?" Charles winked.

"I wasn't flaunting him. Poor Sebastian, I was actually using him. I wanted to make Nick jealous, but it didn't seem to work." I headed back into the kitchen, because I really needed that coffee.

Something good must have gone down, because Charles followed me. "Oh, it worked. He tried hard not to show it, but he didn't like you being with Vampire Boy."

"I wasn't exactly with him."

"Bullshit, you were too with him. So? What was he like?"

Now I was crimson. "I wasn't with him. But we did kiss. And it was…" I patted my chest with my hand.

"That good?"

I just nodded and finished fixing my coffee.

"Now that we have that drama out of the way, you ready to visit with Jackie this morning?"

I sipped my coffee, and I swear just that one sip eased my hangover a bit. "Dude, she's in jail."

"Dude? Dude? Did you really just call me that? If dating a younger guy is going to have you speaking like an idiot teen, I'll have to nip this one fast."

"Whatever." I took another sip of coffee and walked to my office.

Charles failed to mention I'd received a package already this morning.

I walked over to my desk to find a ceramic bowl wrapped in clear cellophane. Inside, I found an assortment of imported coffees, several different sizes and shapes of chocolate bars (all Peruvian chocolate), and a bottle of wine. I pulled back the cellophane to read the wine label more closely.

"Holy shit," I gasped.

Charles leaned against the doorway to my office. "Oh, and you got a package this morning."

I turned to Charles with the bottle in my hand. "Charles, this is a 2005 Chateau Rieussec Sauternes." I shoved the bottle at him.

He took the dessert wine from me, and turned the bottle around, examining it as if he didn't believe me. "Mimi, this cost like a hundred dollars. It's French."

"I know. That's why I covet it, but I've never bought it." I took the bottle back, afraid Charles would sneak it away.

"Who's the package from?" Charles didn't wait for me. He moved past me to the bowl and pulled the card.

He opened the envelope and read to himself. "Oh, barf."

I grabbed for it, but Charles pulled it away. "Give it to me."

He looked at the card again and read aloud. "I wanted you to remember how sweet we were together last night. S."

I snatched the card. I admit it was a bit sappy, but sappy with such good taste. "Barf would be in order if he'd sent a crunch bar and a Riesling, but this," I lifted up a Peruvian chocolate bar, "is very romantic."

"Who would've guessed that inked up boy would have such refined taste?" Charles helped himself to one of the chocolate bars. "Mmmmm."

I slapped his hand as he grabbed for another bar. "Hey, you didn't make out with him last night, I did." I rearranged the chocolate bars as I put the bottle of wine back inside the cellophane.

With chocolate still melting in his mouth, Charles said, "Before we go visit with Jackie, I want you to take a look at something."

"Something good?"

"Nick dropped off a flash drive from William's work computer. They went by his office last night, and the general manager let them make a copy of William's hard drive."

Interesting.

I grabbed the chocolate from Charles and took a bite as we headed to his office. Just as I sat in the chair next to him at the desk, Gemma poked her head in.

"Good morning." She looked around. "Where's Jackie?"

Charles and I looked at each other. I said, "Oh, this isn't a meeting. Charles and I are working on a new case."

Gemma's mood dimmed. "Oh, so no meeting again today?"

Charles looked over his shoulder at Gemma. "Nope, we had it already. You're late."

I smacked Charles on the shoulder. "No, Gemma, you're not late. Something came up with Jackie, so she's not coming in today."

"Oh." Gemma stepped back as if to leave, then stopped. "So what's this new case?"

Charles ignored the question. I thought about doing the same, but I didn't want her to walk in and look over our shoulders. "It's not really a new case. Well, it is, but it's sort of for our eyes only."

Gemma turned on her heel and left without saying anything. I heard a murmur as she stomped down the hall. "None of your fucking business Gemma, as usual."

"Great, now I've pissed her off." I started to get up.

Charles grabbed my arm and pulled me back to my seat.

"She'll get over it." He pulled up a social networking page. Suddenly, Gemma was an afterthought.

My stomach did flips as I watched Charles scroll through pages and pages of this predator's networking profile. He claimed to be a high school senior, varsity football player, varsity lacrosse player, and vice-president of his class. He had the pictures and awards to back it up. William had an elaborate plan to suck these girls in. The private messages he'd been sending were flirtatious, boarding on pornographic. I'd stopped reading after the first few, because my coffee was threatening to come back out the way it went in.

"This is sick."

"You haven't seen anything yet." Charles logged out of this account, then logged back in with another email address. "This is even creepier."

I watched as a picture of a girl, who looked to be about seventeen appeared in the profile at the top of the page. "No freaking way, he's preying on boys, too?"

"I don't think so, but he's using this profile to lure others in." Charles prowled around the site some, and stopped on a comment from a younger boy.

I sat back and stopped looking at the computer screen. "But this is all Internet stuff. Couldn't he get in trouble for being on this site at work?"

"I don't know for sure that he logged on at work. I haven't looked into it that much. The date stamps on the site tell me enough. What I got from the flash drive was the logins and passwords." Charles typed in something that brought up another log.

"What's this?"

"His phone logs." Charles slowed the page a bit.

I leaned forward to look. "I think I'm going to vomit."

"Me, too." Charles shut the whole thing down just as Gemma knocked on the open door.

"You have a visitor," Gemma said flatly. She walked away without announcing the visitor.

I sort of hoped it was Sebastian, but at the same time I hoped it wasn't. I didn't know if I was ready to face him. I blushed again just thinking about making out with a man so young. I realized that when I was a high school senior, he was eight years old. I shivered.

Thinking like that was creepy. I had to remember, we were both experienced, consenting adults.

When I walked into the reception area, no one was there. "Gemma?"

"What?"

"You said we had a visitor."

She pointed toward my office without looking up from her file. Oh, yeah, she was still pissed at being left out.

I entered my office and saw Nick standing at the window, looking out toward the front yard. My breath caught. I know it shouldn't have, but it did.

"Hey," I said.

Nick looked back at me. "You got a minute?"

I went to my desk and sat. Just for fun, I pulled out and unwrapped a chocolate. "Would you like one?"

"What is it?" Nick came over to the desk and leaned across.

His freshly showered scent made my mind swirl. The chocolate in my mouth suddenly tasted like him, just the way he'd tasted the night we made out so many months ago.

"Are you going to tell me what it is?" Nick said.

I came out of my aroma-induced trance and handed him a chocolate. "Peruvian chocolates."

Nick took the piece I offered and sniffed. "This smells better than your average chocolate."

"It sure does. Sebastian sent the selection of chocolates and some wine this morning." Oops, did I say that?

Nick handed back the candy. "Smells good, but no thanks."

Charles grabbed the chocolate from Nick's hand. "Then I'll take it."

"So Charles, what did you get?" Nick said.

"I got a piece of chocolate, and Mimi got a nice piece of ass to give her some chocolate." Charles grinned, but Nick didn't think it was so funny.

"What can we do for you, Detective Christianson?" This had to be police business, or he wouldn't have been at Gotcha.

Nick settled into the chair across from me. "What did you get from the flash drive used to gut Garrison's computer?"

"*We* didn't gut his computer." Charles plopped down next to Nick. He had a look that said, "This is going to be fun."

"I can't get anything off of it. His laptop has some very nice security on it. I haven't been able to get past the login."

I watched as Charles savored his chocolate, one small bite at a time, and contemplated Nick's words. "Who else is doing your forensics these days?"

"I'm not at liberty to say." Nick crossed his arms. "What did you find from the work computer?"

Charles mimicked Nick and crossed his arms. "I'm not at liberty to say."

Nick smiled, and looked at me. I smiled back.

Nick pointed at his teeth. "You have some chocolate…"

I ran my tongue over my teeth and resisted the urge to go look in a mirror.

Charles unfolded his arms and leaned in close to Nick. "Damn, you always smell so good."

I nodded.

"Not going to work, Charles," Nick hissed.

"What? You smell good. Jeez." Charles leaned even closer. "You help me, and I'll help you."

"Help you how?"

"Tit for tat. Tell me what you have on the case, and I'll tell you what I've found."

Nick looked at me again. I didn't even bother to smile. Mostly because I wasn't sure I'd gotten all of the chocolate off my teeth.

Charles broke the silence. "I'll even help you get into his laptop."

Nick blew out a breath. "The M.E. says he was bludgeoned with something that had a pattern, like a lead crystal vase, or carved wood."

"So, the so called weapon in the back of my truck, wasn't the murder weapon?" I spat the words.

"It was a murder weapon, all right," Charles said, before Nick could answer. "I killed a freaking cat with it."

I was appalled. "What?"

"Someone ran over the cat in the street, but it wasn't dead. I couldn't watch it suffer, so I bashed its head in." Charles looked sickened by the memory.

"Yes, that's what the lab tests revealed. It was cat hair and blood on the bat."

I was livid. "So let Jackie out of jail!"

Nick glowered. "I don't tell you how to do your job, don't tell me how to do mine."

Charles made a T sign with his hands. "Time out, children."

We both stared at Charles. He'd shut us up.

"There is still the issue of Jackie's prints in several places in the house."

"We were headed to see her this morning. Is that possible?" Charles had relaxed a bit, too.

"Sure, but can we take care of this information first?"

"The only thing I've found so far is the logins and passwords to his social accounts. He's got several aliases that he uses to flirt with tweens and teens. Seems he likes twelve to fourteen-year-olds."

"Sick bastard." I didn't realize I'd said it aloud until Nick looked at me.

"I just don't understand how a pedophile's mind works. I look at girls that age, and the way their parents let them dress, and I think, 'Put some clothes on,' not 'Wow, I'd like to see you naked.'"

"I didn't even think, 'Wow, I want to see you naked,' when I was their age." Charles tried to lighten the moment.

"Tell us something we don't know."

Nick stood. "I'll meet you at the station. You can talk to Jackie. Maybe she knows something she's not telling me. And then we can get a look at Garrison's laptop."

"I'll set up a flash drive so you'll have all of his login information. There's a lot more there than just what Mimi and I saw this morning."

Nick and I snapped our heads in Charles's direction at the same time. In stereo we said, "There is?"

CHAPTER 9

When the police officer opened the cell Jackie was in, I ran in and hugged her tight. She hugged me back, but didn't say anything. I could feel her shaking. I said, "I'm sorry."

She pulled away and looked at me. "Nothing to be sorry for. How are the twins?"

"They're good. I picked them up and took them to my house. I told them you were working on a job, wouldn't get home until late, and you couldn't call from where you were."

"And they believed you?" She laughed.

"Probably not, but I bribed them with pizza, and all was good."

"Thanks for taking care of them." I could see a tear in her eye.

"It's good for me to see what I'm not missing." After a night with teens, I wasn't so sure about being a mom.

"It's a hard life, but someone has to procreate."

"We couldn't find anything to get you released, and Nick swore you were spending the night, no matter what." I looked behind me to see if Nick was in range. "He's being such an ass."

Jackie sat on the cot and patted the seat next to her. I sat down. The cot was more comfortable than I expected, but I wouldn't want to sleep on it.

"Nick's just doing his job." She smiled a bit. "Did he talk to you last night?"

"Yeah, he came by to make sure I wasn't mad about you being detained, which of course I was." Just thinking about it made my blood boil.

"Did he talk to you about anything else?" Jackie's smile broadened.

I just looked at her. I had no idea what she was getting at.

"He brought me General Tso's chicken last night, along with some pork fried rice. I thought maybe he asked you about my favorite takeout food."

Maybe he wasn't such an ass after all. "Charles must have told him. He didn't have much to say to me. Sebastian stopped by while he was there."

"So I heard. He bought enough dinner for two, and we talked about you and Sebastian while we ate."

I nearly choked on my own spit. "Excuse me?"

Jackie laughed. "Oh girl, he's got it bad for you."

"No, he's got it bad for his new partner. You've seen her; she's a goddess. I hate her." I had to stop thinking like that. Hate is a very bad thing.

Jackie shook her head. "Don't be so sure about that. He asked me a hundred questions about what you've been doing in the last few months, how long you've been seeing 'Vampire Boy,' and what the hell you see in him."

Now I was smiling. "What did you tell him?"

"I said your private life is your business. And then I explained that he had a chance, but he disappeared right after the Bailey murder. That maybe he should have stayed around a bit, wooing you with his good looks, and servicing you the way you need it. Then you wouldn't have to get your sex from a vampire wannabe."

"Please tell me you didn't say I was having sex with Sebastian." Secretly, I hoped she did.

"I didn't come right out and say it, but I implied it. I hope that was okay." She bumped me with her shoulder.

"Whatever. Nick is the past, just like he was all those years ago. I'm not letting him get to me again." I stood. "So, let's get out of here."

Jackie didn't move. "Honey, I'm stuck here for the duration, remember? They think I bashed that creep's head in."

I grabbed her hand and pulled her up. "Not anymore. They have your prints at the scene, but that's it. We are outta here."

Jackie jumped up and hugged me tight. "Really? I'm a free woman?"

I grabbed her and held her at arm's distance. "Besides, you need a shower in a big way."

I stood with Jackie as she signed her release papers, then an officer escorted us to the homicide division, where Nick and Charles were dissecting a laptop.

Charles's head was down close to the computer screen, as if he was listening for something.

"Anything?" Nick asked. He looked flustered.

Charles looked up. "Too many distractions and way too much background noise. I just can't get it."

"I thought you could break into any computer," Nick mocked.

"This guy is good. I mean he's got, or had, his life to protect. I'm sure he has blocks and firewalls in layers. I just can't get through them without my diagnostic equipment." Charles slammed the laptop shut.

"Well, beating up the computer isn't going to make it give up its secrets," Jackie said.

Charles's mood did a one-eighty. "Sweetie!" He jumped up and hugged her. "Orange is *so not* your color."

Jackie squeezed Charles tight and whispered in his ear. "I will never even look at this color again."

Everyone, including Nick, laughed.

Then Nick had to go and ruin the moment. "Don't go out of town, Jackie."

Jackie stepped away from Charles and walked over and kissed Nick on the cheek. "Thanks for everything. I'm guessing that was the nicest stay anyone ever had in one of those cells."

Nick looked down at his paperwork. "Sure."

I wanted to be mad at Nick, but everyone was making it so difficult, especially Jackie, and she's the one who should've been the maddest.

"I'm going to talk to Catey, just like I said I would. There won't be any sweeping this under the rug."

Nick looked up and past us. I turned in the direction he was staring. Piper had walked into the homicide division, her face grim.

She leaned in close to Nick's ear and whispered, "We have a problem."

Nick jumped up from his chair. "You three, stay here. Don't go anywhere." Then directly to me, "And don't go nosing through my stuff."

Who, me?

Nick followed Piper from the room. I think Jackie, Charles and I were too scared to speak. The look on Piper's face told a terrifying tale.

Minutes later, Nick came back, without Piper. His skin was ashen.

"Charles, can I see you alone for a minute?"

Charles looked at me, as if questioning if I was okay with it. I took Jackie by the arm, and we walked out to the main room of the cop shop.

Jackie leaned in close. "What the hell?"

I looked over my shoulder at the closed door. "Not sure, but I know it's not good. Did you see his face?"

Piper approached with two cups of coffee. "Ladies."

Too stunned to refuse, we both took the cups. "Thanks." I wrapped my hands around the paper cup.

Piper whispered, "There's a girl missing."

Jackie sat hard against the table next to us. "Please tell me it's not what I think."

"I shouldn't be telling you this, but they ran the logs on the girl's cell phone. William Garrison's phone number was on the log. The girl has been missing since yesterday."

Jackie stood abruptly, knocking over her coffee, but completely ignoring the mess. "She's been missing more than a day, and the parents are just now calling about it?"

Piper gestured to a rookie cop, "Hey, Stewart, can you get some paper towels over here?"

Stewart, moving at the pace of January molasses, went for the paper towels.

Piper sat at the table, so Jackie and I sat, too. "No, she's been in the system since yesterday. She's not the runaway type, so we put out a BOLO as soon as the parents called. There's been an Amber Alert out since yesterday. They just found the match on the cell phone logs and called me."

"How did they know to call you?" I asked.

"The name William Garrison is on everyone's lips, so when the match came through…"

"Where's the bathroom?" Jackie could barely stand up straight.

Piper grabbed the paper towels from Stewart. "Take her to the bathroom, quickly."

Stewart half-glared at Piper as he took Jackie by the elbow and led her to the bathroom.

"Does this mean…" I felt sick, but I wasn't going to show it.

"We don't know what it means. Garrison may have nothing to do with the girl's disappearance." She didn't look like she felt it in her bones.

Before Jackie came back from the bathroom, Charles exited the homicide division with Garrison's laptop, and Nick, in tow.

"We need to get a move on. Suddenly, time is of the essence." Charles bolted past me toward the entrance of the police station.

Piper glanced at Nick, then at Charles. "Um, chain of evidence?"

Nick said, "Don't worry about it."

Piper stood to full height, stepped in front of Charles before he got to the door. "Hold up." To Nick she said, "You aren't going to fuck this up. We need a chain of evidence."

"Look, Detective, I've been doing this a lot longer than you have, and I'm your senior officer, so don't tell me how to do my job." I swear Nick hissed.

Lots of people seemed to be telling Nick how to do his job lately.

Charles stepped between them. "Detective Mason, I have a contract with the Salinas Police Department. I've been doing computer forensics on a freelance basis for several years now. Detective Christianson and I understand the importance of the chain of evidence."

Nick glared at Piper. "Detective Ambrossen undersigned the evidence sheet. Charles is the best at what he does."

"Why can't he just do what he's so good at right here?"

I decided to defuse the situation. "Detective Mason, Charles has more equipment at our offices. He's having problems, just like the other tech, getting past Garrison's lockdown of this computer. At the office, he has tools and such that can get past it."

Nick and Charles walked out together. Piper watched them go, the red in her face fading.

"That asshole. Why didn't he just tell me that?" Tears welled in her eyes.

"Because he's Nick, and he prides himself on being an asshole. It's even worse when you're sleeping with him." I really should have left that last part off, but it was out there and I couldn't take it back.

"You're having sex with him?" Piper asked, incredulous.

I laughed. "No." Maybe a tad bit defensive.

"Then what are you talking about?"

Jackie was back from the bathroom. "She thinks you're doing it with Nick."

Piper's eyes widened. "Doing what?"

I shot Jackie a look. *What the fuck?*

Jackie looked at Piper like she was an alien. "Having sex, silly."

Piper nearly doubled over laughing. "Oh, honey, the only penis shaped thing I've ever had was made of silicone and hot pink."

I stood there, speechless. Yeah, I know, hard to believe.

Now Jackie was laughing too.

I said, "Oh my God, I should've seen it."

Suddenly, Piper wasn't laughing anymore. "Excuse me?"

"Charles. He knew from the moment he met you. I wondered why he was so attracted to you. So helpful."

"Helpful?" Piper asked.

"At the crime scene, when you had barfed. He was so caring and even gave you his shirt."

Jackie stopped laughing and deadpan, said, "Charles gave someone the shirt off his back? Surely you jest."

"I jest you not," I said. "That's what I mean. Charles has never done a chivalrous thing for a female in his life."

Jackie interjected, "That's not completely true. He's pretty good to you and me."

I had to agree. "Most of the time."

Charles popped back into the room. It was like he knew we were talking about him.

"Ladies, let's go. There's a life…" He caught himself before he said too much.

Thoughts going back to the missing girl, we sobered up fast, and Jackie and I scooted toward the door.

Piper called after us, "Hey, God speed." Then she winked at Charles. He winked back.

CHAPTER 10

Charles was snappier than usual when we got back to the office, so Jackie and I decided to leave him alone with Gemma, who was still sulking.

Normally Gemma would be in on the case, but I needed her to pick up the slack on other clients and cases. I'd left her a long list of tasks, so she'd be busy, and not completely left out.

Jackie had wanted to keep Catey's improprieties between us. She was embarrassed enough that we were involved.

"How long before Catey gets out of school?" I asked.

"Now, as far as I'm concerned. I let her get away with not telling me everything." Jackie sniffed her armpits. "I should probably shower, but I want to get to the bottom of this. I don't smell like a homeless person yet, so do you want to come with me?"

"Shouldn't you two work this out in private?" I really wanted to go.

"You were with her when she started her period. It doesn't get much more private than that." Jackie grabbed me by the arm. "Let's go."

I snagged my handbag as I let her drag me out of the office.

"Besides, I may need you for moral support. You always were able to be a bit blunter about things than I was." Jackie waited at the passenger door to the Land Rover.

I guess I was driving. "Ouch, that kinda stings."

Jackie got in the car and said, "It wasn't a slight. I wish I could speak more bluntly to my kids. It's just that, I don't know, I guess it's harder to talk to your own kids than it is to someone else's."

I understood what she meant. Not many parents got jazzed about the idea of talking to their kids about sex and drugs.

As I drove toward the school, I said, "I'll just be a fly on the wall."

Jackie laughed hard. "That'll be the day."

"That stung, too."

I sat in the driver's seat and waited at the loading zone while Jackie went into the school to get Catey. I drummed my fingers on the steering wheel to the beat of the song on my CD. I was so into it that I jumped when I heard the tapping on my window.

I rolled down the window. "Are you following me?"

Nick smiled. "Maybe."

Damn, he looked good. He'd changed clothes and was wearing a white T-shirt with a navy sweater vest. Not many men can pull of this look, but Nick could. I remained casual, though my heart was thumping. "What's up?"

"What are you doing right now?" He leaned in closer to the window.

"You do know there's this thing called a cell phone, right? You could've just called me." But I was really glad to have him there in the flesh.

"Yeah, I know. But I was driving down this street and saw your car. Are you busy?"

So it was random, he wasn't following me. I felt much better that he just happened to see my car.

"I'm waiting for Jackie. She decided to take Catey out of school and have a talk with her now. Being that time is of the essence, she wants to know if anything Catey knows will help the missing girl."

"We don't even know that the two are related," Nick said.

"But if they are, this can only help." I looked past Nick and saw Jackie walking out of the administration building with Catey in tow.

Nick looked back, following my gaze. "I'll leave you be. Can you call me later tonight? I'd really like to talk."

Really? Seriously? We hadn't spoken in months until this incident, and now he wanted me to call? "You have my number. Call me later if you aren't too busy."

Nick grinned and stepped away from the window. Jackie and Catey walked up as Nick turned and walked away. He looked back and waved, but didn't talk to them.

I slammed my hand down on my steering wheel. "Damn."

"What's the matter, Aunt Mimi?" Catey climbed in shotgun.

Jackie got in the back seat. I immediately saw her strategy. I was such a sucker.

"Nothing. I'm just being stupid." I rubbed my wrist where I'd hit the steering wheel with the little bone that sticks out.

"Yeah, boys will do that to a girl." Catey looked over her shoulder at her mom.

I put the car in gear and started driving.

Jackie piped up right away. "Speaking of boys, or men, as the case may be--"

Catey whined, "Mom? Really? Here?"

Jackie snapped. "Yes, here. And your Aunt Mimi is here to be sure I don't let you pull one over on me again."

"Pull one over? What does that even mean?" Catey said, now whining even more.

I could see Jackie bracing herself. "Remember how we talked yesterday about being careful with the people you talk to online, and who you let have your phone number?"

"I told you I'd be more careful. And I'm sorry I was so secretive, but I promise I'm done with that." Catey turned in her seat and was leaning against the passenger door.

"Well, what I didn't tell you is that the boy you've been texting and chatting with sent you a pic of his penis."

"What? How would you even know that?" Catey snapped.

"I had your phone, remember?" Jackie didn't back off from the barrage she knew would come.

"You said you changed your mind, that you trusted me, Mom!"

"Oh, stop with the whining already!" I pointed to Catey. "You chill." Then to Jackie, I said, "You just zip it for a moment."

They both looked stunned, but did as I said.

"Yes, Catey, we saw your laptop and your cell phone. So what if some of the texts were a bit racy? You thought the guy was seventeen, after all. I mean, if

I'd have had a cell phone when I was your age - okay, well, we won't go there."

Catey's eyes welled with tears, but I kept going while I was on a roll.

"Do you understand that predators like this William Garrison guy are doing this to more than just one girl?"

Catey shook her head. "What does Anna Garrison's dad have to do with any of this?"

I looked at Jackie. Had I said too much?

Catey sniffled and wiped at her tears. "What is she talking about, Mom?"

Jackie sat up. "The supposed boy you were sexting? Honey, that boy was actually Mr. Garrison."

Catey's face lost all color. "Are you two nuts? Mr. Garrison is Anna's dad."

"I know who he is, I mean, was," Jackie said.

"Was?"

"Let me cut in again. I'm just going to say it, not sugarcoat it. Catey, you are a big girl and you need to know how the real world works." I was ready to dump a load on this poor girl.

"Huh?"

"William Garrison, Anna's dad, was pretending to be this Dylan boy you've been texting, or more like sexting, and chatting with online. He's not only prowling after you, but also other young girls."

Catey went from no color to green. "You mean that cute boy wasn't really a cute boy?" She looked at her mom as a tear rolled down her cheek.

"Catey, sweetie, I know you were at the house. Did you actually see Mr. Garrison?" I needed to get more information before she completely broke down.

"No, I never met with Dylan. I didn't have my phone, so I couldn't text or call him. I remembered his street name, but not the address." She sniffed. "When I told Anna I was meeting him, she freaked out. She said talking and texting was one thing, but meeting a total stranger all by myself was stupid."

"It is," I said.

"I thought Anna was stupid. Oh my gosh, she knew. I think she knew. Anytime I talked about Dylan, she'd act all weird." Catey shivered and wrapped her arms around herself. "I thought she was just jealous."

Jackie sank back into the seat. Her little girl was growing up, and she was learning the hard way. "Okay."

Before this got into territory where a teen was telling me more about sex than I already knew, I spoke up. "I need to know exactly what happened up until your mom took your phone. Every detail."

Catey stiffened. "No way, it's so embarrassing."

I leaned in and spoke low. "Embarrassing or not, I need every last detail. There's a girl missing. She's your age, and she may be one of William's victims."

Catey's eyes went wide. "Really? No. This can't be."

I didn't budge. "Every last detail." Then I sat back in my seat, and waited for Catey to speak.

She took a deep breath. "Where do you want me to start?"

"At the beginning, from the first contact. I need to know how this works." I pulled a recorder from my pocket.

"What the hell?" Only it was Jackie protesting, not Catey.

"I'm going to record this. I don't want to miss any details when we give the information to the police. You can use names, or not, but I need to be recording." I lifted the recorder a bit as if asking, "Okay?"

Catey said, "I'm fine with the recorder, but," she looked into the back seat again, "Mom, will you be okay with hearing the details? Knowing how stupid your daughter is?"

Jackie reached forward and put her hand on Catey's shoulder. "Sweetie, you aren't stupid. These creeps who do this, they are good at it. They have lots of practice, and years of honing their skills."

Catey shook her head. "I was so naïve."

"So let's get started, from the beginning." I pushed record.

"He first friended me on this site I'm always on. We started chatting, and he liked the same music I liked. He even posted videos of my favorite bands, and linked them to me. I was flattered. I mean, no guy had even taken that kind of time to be interested in me and my music.

"Then he sent me a book, via email, an eBook. It was Twilight. He said when he read it, all he could think of was us together." Catey cringed. "Oh God, that should have been a clue. Edward is like 300 years old, and Bella is still in high school. Creepy."

Jackie asked, "Did you read the book?"

"I'd already read it, but I thought it was so cool that he liked it, too. Even though I wasn't a crazed fan, I did like the story. And it just went like that for a while. Next thing I know, I gave him my cell number and we were texting." She pulled out her phone and looked at it.

"So you never talked?" I asked.

"No, I don't like talking on the phone that much. It's so much easier to text, so I'd never heard his voice. But I saw all of the pictures on his page, and knew he was cute. All of his friends were cute, too. There were pictures of him with his dog, and you know how I love dogs."

"Fine, if you promise to never look at another male, I'll get you a dog," Jackie relented, well, sort of.

Catey laughed. "I don't want a dog. Not right now, anyway."

"So," I said.

"So we texted each other for weeks. He was so sweet, and we had so much in common. Then in the last week, it got a little, I don't know, sexy." She looked at us both, pointedly. "You saw the texts."

"Yes, we did," I admitted. "But were you just playing along, or did you really mean those things?"

Catey thought for a moment. "Both, I guess." She hesitated. "I mean, I really wanted him to like me, want me."

Jackie spoke very low. "Oh, Catey."

Catey groaned. "I know, Mom." She started fidgeting with her book bag.

"He invited you to his house?"

"At first, it was just the joking texts. Then he called me."

"So you talked to him?"

Catey looked at Jackie like she'd lost her mind. "No. I just texted him back. But then I started deleting the texts. And he was calling from a different number than the texts. I didn't want him to hear how young I sound."

"What happened when he invited you over?"

Catey crossed her arms again. "It was all innocent. He said he had a bad cold, could I come over and keep him company. He said his mom was out of town, and he was too sick to even make himself some soup. I said I'd be happy to come over and take care of him."

"When was this?"

Catey breathed deep. "Yesterday morning, before Mom took my phone. I was pissed off because I had to let him know I couldn't come by until later because I had a test that morning. And since Mom had my phone, I couldn't text him."

"So how did you end up at his house?" I was so curious how this psycho worked.

Catey sighed again. "I borrowed Alyssa's phone, but I couldn't remember Dylan's, I mean, the number."

I looked at Jackie to see her reaction. "So you weren't at the school when your mom got there?"

"I'm sure I was, I never left. Really." Catey looked at her mom, who gave no reaction.

I had to admit, Jackie was being very calm about all of this. I knew it was killing her. It was killing me, and Catey wasn't even my kid.

"Anyway, he said he was really sick, and wanted some soup. So of course, I wanted to actually go see him. It was sort of exciting. I mean if he was sick, we couldn't make out or anything, but at least I'd get to see him in person." Catey put her head in her hands and rubbed her face.

"I need some air." Jackie opened the car door and got out of the car.

"Mom wasn't really working on a case last night, was she?" Catey said through her hands.

"Nope." I rubbed Catey's back. "She was in jail."

Catey's head snapped up. "Jail? What?"

"Before we go there, I need to know what happened when you got to the house." I was pretty sure I'd lost her, but she answered.

"I never got to the house. I was telling Anna I wanted to go, but she talked me out of it." Catey sighed and rubbed her face again.

I thought of the picture with Catey and her friend on the mantle. If she'd gone in the house, she'd know William was Anna's dad.

"Anna never said she thought Dylan was someone else?"

"No, but she was really weird about it."

"Do you think she knew her dad was a predator?"

"She's the one who introduced us online."

I didn't know what to say about this. Could Anna know about her dad?

Jackie opened the door and climbed in the back seat again. Her color was better now. She breathed in deep, but didn't say anything.

Catey looked at her mom, and continued, "Anna's parents are divorced. He only has supervised visits. But he's friends with Anna on our social page, so I know what he looks like."

"And do you know why he only had supervised visits?" Jackie asked.

Irritated, Catey snapped, "I don't know. Anna and I don't talk about our parents that much. We have more important things on our minds."

I had to laugh.

They both turned to look at me, as if they forgot I was there.

"William Garrison was pretending to be a seventeen-year-old boy. He's a predator," I explained. Then to Jackie, I said, "Do you think he found his victims through his daughter's social pages?"

Catey looked to her mom for confirmation.

Jackie nodded.

Catey suddenly pushed past Jackie and bolted out of the car. Once out, she paced the sidewalk. I could see a jerking movement in her chest. Through the sobbing, I thought I heard her say, "I don't know. I just don't know."

Jackie got out of the car and held her daughter. "Honey, I know this is hard. But there's a problem. William is dead, and there's a girl missing. We aren't sure if they're related. If she was one of the girls William was stalking, we need to find her."

In a heartbeat, Catey was no longer crying. She no longer heaved. Wiping her eyes, she asked, "Is the girl's name Tiffany?"

CHAPTER 11

As much as I didn't want to call Nick, I needed to know more about the girl that disappeared. Was her name Tiffany? Did she go to the same school as Catey?

We got her back in the car, and I took Jackie and Catey straight home. I'd come get Jackie in the morning if she wanted to come to work. For now, she needed to be with her daughter. This was a lot for a young teen to process. On the way home, Catey kept saying, "I really thought I was smarter than that."

She was a smart girl, but this guy had years to hone his "craft." My head was spinning as I drove away from their house. I grabbed my phone and hit the speed dial button. Don't judge me; I know Nick's number shouldn't be in my speed dial.

"Hey, Mimi." Nick sounded genuinely happy to hear from me.

"We really need to talk." I didn't sound as happy, as I was really starting to feel ill.

"I'm working this missing person case," Nick said. "Maybe later tonight?"

"I'm in my car. Where are you? We really need to talk, like now."

Exasperated, Nick said, "Mimi, can't it wait? There is a girl's life at stake here."

"It's about the girl. Is her name Tiffany?"

There was silence on the other end of the phone. "What did Charles tell you?"

I'd been holding my breath. "Charles didn't tell me, Catey did."

Nick's tone turned urgent. "Meet me at your house. How soon can you get there?"

"I'm just pulling into my driveway."

Nick must have gone lights and siren, because he was jogging up my front lawn before I got to the door.

"What's going on?" Nick called as he approached.

"Come on in. I'll make some coffee." I opened the door and went straight to the kitchen.

I had some gourmet beans I'd ground that morning, so I scooped them into the coffee maker and added filtered water. Looking across the counter, I saw the bottle of wine Sebastian and I had shared the night before, and I smiled for a moment, forgetting the present reality.

Nick came behind me, breaking my moment of peace. "So?"

"Jackie and I talked with Catey. We asked her what happened, and she told us everything. When we told her about the missing girl, she asked if her name was Tiffany."

"Tiffany Anderson," Nick stated flatly.

"Tiffany Anderson," I repeated. "Have you heard anything from Charles?"

"He called just before you did. He's having a hell of a time getting into Garrison's computer."

"Charles?" I couldn't believe it.

"The man had a lot to lose if he was caught. He wanted to be sure he didn't get caught. For all we know, everything on the drive could be wiped clean if the wrong password is entered too many times."

"Did Charles tell you that?"

"Yes. He's waiting to get some sort of tool from the Naval Postgraduate School. He said one of the officers is trying to get it from an Army base in Kentucky."

"Why don't we have this tool?" I'd paid a lot of money for Charles to have the best computer forensics tools available.

"Apparently, it's something new. Charles said something about it being in beta." Nick reached in front of me, grabbed a coffee cup from the rack, and poured himself a cup.

I didn't move, enjoying the close proximity. I resisted the urge to move closer.

Nick finished filling the coffee cup and walked to the table. He sat and stared at the cup.

"What's going on?" I'd never seen him like this. Not that I'd seen a lot of him lately.

"This case is killing me. I need to find a killer I don't want to arrest. I want to find him and give him an award. But then again, I want to find him and strangle him." Nick sipped his coffee carefully to avoid burning his mouth.

"Strangle him? Why?" I didn't understand. The killer had taken a predator off the streets.

"Because, if William were still alive, he could tell us where to find Tiffany." Realizing the coffee wasn't too hot, he took a bigger drink. "This is good."

"European coffee beans."

"What's with you and all of this foreign food stuff? Peruvian chocolate, French wine, European coffee. Whatever happened to good old fashioned Chardonnay, Folgers, or Nestlé's?"

"It's called expanding your palate." I poured coffee for myself. "Besides, it's delicious."

Nick took another sip and nodded his agreement.

"So, let me tell you what Catey told us. It might help." I said, and then remembered I had the recording. "No, wait."

I ran out to my car, got the recorder, and ran back in. I was a bit winded, so I made a mental note to add running back into my regular routine.

"Here." I tried to disguise the panting.

"What's this?" Nick turned the recorder over in his hand.

"It's a recording of my conversation with Catey. I got her permission to record what she said, so I wouldn't miss anything." I pointed to the flippy thing. I had no idea what it was called, but it was the male end of the USB port. "This flips out, so you can plug into a USB port on your computer and download the recording. So when you're done with it, I'd like the recorder back."

Nick tossed the tiny recorder up in the air, snagged it, and put it in his pocket. "This is great, thanks. I don't know if it'll help, but it's something."

Nick's cell phone rang and he answered it before the end of the first ring.

I waited as he sat for a moment and said nothing, just listened. He stood abruptly and poured out the rest of his coffee in the sink. Then he rinsed the cup, still not saying a word.

I started to feel uncomfortable in the silence, as he never even muttered "Uh huh" or anything.

He looked at me, as he walked out of the kitchen. "Okay, I'll meet CSU at the scene."

He flipped his phone shut and put it in his pocket.

"Okay, so I guess you'll let me know if Catey's story helps?"

"Sure," he mumbled. "We're going back to Garrison's house. The lab tech got a sample of Tiffany's hair. We're going to see if we can find any match at Garrison's house. It's a long shot, but we have to try. I just know these two cases are linked."

I wanted to be able to do something, too. "Give me back the recorder. I'll give it to Charles, and he can upload it. I'll have him send it to your email account, or your phone, if you can do that."

"Have him do it right away, and I need him to call me. Are you headed over there now?" He handed it to me, and our flesh brushed at the wrist.

I wanted to grab his wrist and pull him in close. But before I could do anything, he grabbed my waist and pulled me in close. I didn't even fight him; I was too shocked to respond.

He leaned in close, and I thought he was going to kiss me. I closed my eyes.

"Be very careful with Sebastian," he whispered in my ear. Then he stepped away from me.

My internal temperature skyrocketed, and not just from Nick's close proximity. I couldn't believe I thought he was going to kiss me. I mean, with all he had on his mind, what was wrong with me? Wishful thinking in a big, bad way.

"Thanks for the warning. But I think I know him a bit better than you do."

"Don't be so sure." Nick turned and walked out the door.

When the door closed, I stomped my foot hard on the floor, like a spoiled child. "Idiot," I said aloud. "Oh, jeez, how could I be so stupid?" I stamped my other foot, went to the cabinet to grab a travel mug, and poured myself another cup of coffee.

I pocketed the recorder and headed for the office.

***

Gemma was nowhere to be found when I arrived at the office, though her car was in the parking lot. I walked past the reception area and went straight to Charles's office.

He sat ramrod straight, which is his "things aren't going well" position when he's working on a problem. I was almost afraid to approach him. I decided that instead of asking how it was going, since I knew it was bad, I'd offer up information.

"I've got something for you," I said, as I stepped behind him.

He didn't jump, but he definitely stiffened. Without turning around to acknowledge me, he said, "What do you have?"

I leaned around him and set the recorder on the desk. I came around and hopped up on his desk. I was trying to lighten the mood, but the look on his face told me to get off the desk before he pushed me off. I slid off until I was leaning against it.

"Jackie and I pulled Catey out of school and had a talk with her." I pointed. "That's a recording of our conversation."

Charles smiled. "Do you think there's anything that will help find that little girl?"

"She's not that little, Charles, she's in Catey's grade."

"Compared to us, she's a little girl." He leaned back, relaxing a bit. "Were they friends?"

"According to Catey, Anna's father was friends with her on their social network. She thinks maybe that's how he contacted her."

"So, is Tiffany friends with Catey and Anna?"

"Well, even if they aren't friends in person, they probably are on the 'net."

Charles was right back at the computer, only this time it was his computer he was typing away on. "If I can get Tiffany's information, maybe we can see what transpired."

"How do we do that?"

"I'm getting her parents' address now. We can go have a talk with them. Maybe Nick can meet us there. To make it easier, I need to use her computer to log into the sites." Charles stood and grabbed a sweater from the back of his chair.

"I'm going with you. I'll call Nick on the way." I rushed after Charles.

Gemma was sitting at reception as we left. "You have four or five messages from Sebastian."

"Do you have his number?"

She handed me a slip of paper. I looked at it. Did I really want to call him? I thought about it on the way to the car. Yes, I did. But the next number I dialed was Nick's.

"We're on our way to see Tiffany's parents. Charles wants you to meet us there." I waited for a reprimand to stay out of police business.

"It's going to take me a few minutes before I can leave here. I'll call ahead and let the officer at the house know who you are, in case I don't get there for awhile." Nick sounded rushed. "Gotta go."

"Nick's going to call ahead, so the officer at the house knows we're coming. He wants you to start without him." I disconnected the call, but I didn't put my phone away. I dialed again.

"Who are you calling now?" Charles asked.

"Hey, what's up?" I said, into the phone. "Gemma said you called."

I could hear the smile in Sebastian's voice. "I just wanted to be sure you got my package, and that everything is cool with us."

I chuckled. "Everything with us is perfect. And yes, I got the package. Thanks so much for the wonderful chocolates and wine."

He laughed. "Did you get the note?"

I blushed. "Yes, and thanks. Sorry I didn't get back to you earlier. We've had a crazy day around here."

"I remember you said things were crazy last night."

I thought I'd make the next move. "What are you doing tonight?"

There was silence on the other end of the line. "Look, I've gotta go. I'll call you later. Is this your cell phone number?"

Oh my God, I was getting the brush off. This was completely humiliating. I hung up without responding.

Within seconds, I had a text.

CHAPTER 12

"Nick's on his way right now."

"How do you know this?" Charles parked in front of Tiffany's parents' home.

"Text." I showed him the phone.

"Should we wait here for him, or go ahead on in?" Charles gathered up his bag of "tricks" from behind his seat.

"I vote go." The sooner we had answers, the better.

We got out of the car, but both of us stalled. This had to be so hard for parents: not knowing was harder than knowing, no matter how bad. As we walked up the pathway to the front door, a woman opened the door and came running out. The house was one of those McMansions erected before the real estate bubble burst.

"Are you from the agency?" She sounded desperate and hopeful at once.

"I'm Charles Parks and this is Mimi Capurro, the owner of Gotcha Detective Agency. We're here to take a look at your daughter's computer." Charles offered his hand.

"I'm Julie Anderson." She shook his hand as we kept walking toward the door. "Thanks for getting here so fast."

I just smiled and followed behind. This was out of my league, so I was here for backup. My smile turned into a gasp as we entered the double door entryway.

There are foyers that are amazing, and there are foyers that take your breath away. This one had light grey marble tiles with antiques placed expertly to show their age and grace. I noticed the hall tree first. The oak wood was polished to its natural sheen, and next to it was an umbrella stand. I've seen homes with antique overkill, but this was tasteful. Julie led us to a room off to the right.

"This is our library." She opened the door to a room larger than my house. "We don't allow the kids to have their computers in their rooms. That way they aren't being secretive about their online activity. I thought we were being smart."

We walked into a room with three separate seating areas, all with a couch, two club chairs and a desk. Each area had its own flower arrangement, like the kind you see in five star hotels. All three desks had laptop and tabletop computers. *Can we say computer overkill?* One wall was floor to ceiling bookshelves, loaded with books.

"Well, hello everyone," Charles said. He was speaking to the two uniformed officers and three women already in the room.

One of the women stood. "Tim went into the kitchen to see what's taking Maria so long with the coffee."

Julie pointed to the women. "These are my sisters: Eva, Baylee, and Morgan." Each woman lifted a perfectly manicured hand when Julie said her name. They were similar versions of the same woman. About five foot six, less than a hundred pounds, platinum blonde bobs, and perfectly applied makeup. The only thing differentiating them was a minimal number of years and their impeccable clothing. They all wore pencil skirts, showing off their tanned and toned legs to their best advantage, and a silk blouse, different colors and patterns, of course.

I felt like I was in a version of Stepford Wives, but it should be called the Stepford Sisters. It felt surreal. I just put my hand up and waved. I was afraid if I engaged in conversation, I'd walk out of the house looking like Barbie with a bob.

"Ladies, lovely to meet you, but this isn't a social call." Charles turned to Julie. "Tiffany's computer?"

Too much estrogen in a room made Charles queasy.

Julie led Charles and me to the desk on the far side of the room. Suddenly, there was a line behind us, following us to the desk.

Charles looked back. "I'm sorry, Mrs. Anderson, but I can't work with so many people in the room."

Julie didn't hesitate. She flicked her hand to the women and the police, "Out. Now. You heard him, he needs space."

With that, everyone filed neatly from the room. As they left, Nick walked in.

"I see you've met the Stepford Sisters," he said, as he crossed the room.

I swallowed hard, stunned that he used the very words I'd been thinking. "They're very nice."

"Yes, they're well trained," he said, as he moved past me to Charles, who was already implementing his hacking skills.

I leaned over Charles's shoulder. "Well, anything?"

Still typing, Charles said, "Nick smells better than you do. Can you switch places?"

Nick didn't move. I didn't, either. Charles sighed.

I watched as he worked his magic and blew right through the passwords. He was in Tiffany's social accounts and checking out the private messages. Smack dab at the top of the page, Dylan had sent her a message.

"Hey cutie, my plans fell through. I'm stuck at home today. Come see me. We can get nasty just like you showed me in your pictures."

"This isn't good." Charles went into Tiffany's photos.

This girl wasn't some innocent teen. There were photos of her doing a beer bong, at least I'm assuming it was beer. Scrolling down, she'd send Dylan photos of herself naked. Her hands covered her jungle and her boobs, but not much was left to the imagination. She was a bit pudgy, quite unlike her mother and aunts. I hate to say it, but she wasn't exactly cute. She'd been giving it everything she had in those photos. She wanted Dylan to want her.

Nick looked away. "Bet she just loved the attention. She's sending him pictures."

Charles said, "Well, since they're friends, I can look at Dylan's page, too."

"I thought you already did." He'd been in Catey's computer.

"I have, but I didn't hack into his account." Charles logged out of Tiffany's account, then logged into Dylan's. "Just need to adjust my tool."

"By all means, don't let the fact that we're standing here stop you." Nick grinned.

Charles pointed to the black stick on the side of the computer. "This tool, you tool."

We all laughed, and then realized where we were and cut it short.

"I'm in," Charles said.

"That's what he said." Well, they were getting all perverted. I wanted to be one of the boys too.

"Nick? Did you say that to Mimi?"

I could've shot Charles that very moment.

Nick lightly punched Charles in the shoulder. "I don't kiss and tell."

Suddenly, Charles wasn't joking around anymore. He leaned in closer to the screen. "Do you see that?"

Nick and I leaned in close. I could feel his breath on my neck. My vision blurred for a second, while my body processed this feeling.

"See what?" Nick leaned even closer to the screen.

"Right there." Charles pointed to a girl next to Dylan in a party picture. "That's Anna."

"She knows," Nick said.

"Catey did say Anna was really weird about her and Dylan." I couldn't believe it. It didn't make sense.

"First, let's be clear," Charles said. "We agree that William is Dylan, and that Dylan and Tiffany definitely had connections. So this means Tiffany may have been William's last victim before he was killed."

"So where is she?" This thought made me cringe. If William hadn't been killed, maybe Tiffany would be safe.

Nick's cell phone rang.

"Let's get out of here. I'm going to take the laptop with me." Charles packed up his tools and closed Tiffany's laptop. He slipped it into his bag along with the rest of his stuff.

Nick had moved across the room to take his call, so I just followed Charles out of the library.

"Hold up," Nick said to us, and then went back to his call.

I stopped, but Charles kept walking. I heard him approach someone in the foyer.

"You realize you did this to your daughter," Charles snapped.

I heard a man's voice. "Excuse me?"

Charles's voice was low and full of rage. "You thrive on perfection. Tiffany wasn't perfect. Nothing she did was going to make her cute enough to fit into this family. So she started looking elsewhere for love and attention."

"What the hell?" It was Julie this time.

"And you, with your plastic face and plastic personality. What do you think you're teaching your poor daughter? You fed her insecurity and drove her to search for approval from a *boy* she met online."

"You have no right to talk to my wife like this," Tim growled.

"I'm not just talking to your wife. If your daughter is gone, then you did this to her, too. Because I've got news for you, the boy she was showing her naked pictures to was a man, and that man is now dead. So the chances of finding your daughter just got slimmer." He was no longer speaking low; Charles was in full rage.

Nick came running from the library into the foyer. I could tell he wanted to stop Charles from saying more, but he wanted this family to know what they'd done to their daughter.

I thought about Catey. Did Jackie make her feel inferior? I didn't think that was the case with Catey. They had been sexting each other, but she hadn't sent any pictures.

Nick waited a few more seconds before he grabbed Charles by the arm. He looked at the Andersons. "I'm sorry about this. We're leaving."

Charles yanked his arm free. "I wasn't finished."

Now Nick locked onto Charles's forearm. "Yes. You. Are." He nearly dragged him from the house.

Once we were outside, Nick let go of Charles. I walked a few steps behind them, knowing what happened when Charles blew a cork.

Behind me, I heard Tim Anderson say, "She was sending naked photos of herself to a man?"

I shook my head and kept walking.

"They needed to know. That Barbie doll, with her skin stretched across her skull, made her daughter feel fat and ugly." Charles almost whispered.

"How do you know that?" Nick asked.

"I just know." Charles walked away. He got in his car and left skid marks on the street as he drove away.

Nick looked at me. "Need a ride?"

I stared after the Spyder. "I guess I do."

CHAPTER 13

The tension from Charles's tirade was still thick in the air as Nick drove me back to my office. Nick and I didn't talk much. I looked out the window, trying to figure out what in Charles's past made him react this way.

"Do you think Charles had issues with his parents?"

"Oh, Charles has had plenty of issues. His parents were the least of his problems when he was growing up. But I do think he got his fastidiousness from his family."

"I can't say that he's wrong. His method of delivering the message may have been wrong, but he's right." Nick maneuvered his car into a parking lot.

"Sorry about Charles. When he gets up on his soapbox, you never know what's going to happen."

Just as I was about to get out of the car, Nick put his hand on my forearm. "What do you think about Anna being in that picture with the real Dylan?"

"I just don't see how she could possibly be involved. Maybe William saw her with the picture, and decided to borrow the real Dylan's pictures."

"William is friends with Anna on a social networking site all of the kids are on these days."

"Stay here just a minute, I'll be right back." I didn't wait for Nick to respond and got out of the car.

I was back out in the parking lot within minutes, and to my surprise, Nick was still there.

"What would you say about going to have a talk with Anna?"

The look of surprise on Nick's face was priceless. "I take it you have some information you haven't shared with me yet. We've been trying to find the girl."

I climbed in this car and buckled my seatbelt. "Jackie was able to get Anna's cell phone number for me."

"What good will that do? You think if we call, she'll tell us where she is, and then be waiting for us?"

"I wasn't so sure about that, so Jackie had Catey call Anna to see where she's at, and she's at her aunt's house."

Nick leaned over and kissed me on the cheek. "Have I told you lately that you rock?"

I handed him a piece of paper with the address.

Luckily, Anna didn't live far from the Gotcha offices, and we were there within minutes.

"Do you want me to stay in the car?" I asked, even though I was unbuckling my seatbelt.

"No, I think you deserve to come with me on this one. But please, let me do the talking, at least at first."

Not wanting to look a gift horse in the mouth, I followed quietly behind Nick as we walked to the front door.

The neighborhood and the house were definitely for a lower income bracket than that of the Anderson family. I was pretty sure this house didn't have a foyer or a library. It took everything I had not to peek through the window as we waited for somebody to answer the door.

The woman who eventually answered the door was average looking, average height and mousy brown hair, but somehow cute. She wore a plain white blouse with a plaid skirt that fit nicely, and hugged her hips.

"Yes," she said, with a voice that sounded like she'd been crying.

Nick smiled and flashed his badge. "We're here to speak to Anna Garrison."

The woman's face hardened. "Can I help you with something? Anna isn't available."

Nick introduced himself to the woman, who happened to be Stephanie Garrison, William's sister, and Anna's aunt.

I know Nick told me to sit back and be quiet, but I thought maybe this situation needed a woman's touch. So I stepped forward and offered my hand. "Hi, Ms. Garrison, I'm Mimi Capurro. It really is imperative that we speak with Anna."

Stephanie looked behind her into the house, stepped outside and closed the door. "Before you talk to her, do you mind if we go for a walk?"

She didn't wait for an answer, and continued walking towards the sidewalk. Nick and I followed like obedient puppies. Once we caught up to her on the sidewalk, she started talking.

"I'm sorry about your brother," I said, though I wasn't really sorry.

"Look, I knew someday I'd have to have this conversation, and I knew it wasn't going to be an easy one. You see, I'm the one you should be arresting."

Nick tensed. "Ms. Garrison, if you're the one who killed William Garrison, then I would be more than happy to arrest you."

"I should've killed him. The thing is, I've known about William since I was a little girl. I'm his sister, and I'm pretty sure I was his first victim."

I stopped walking. Of all of the things this woman could have said, this was the last thing I expected to hear. William had started his career as a child molester with his own sister.

"Ms. Garrison, I'm so sorry to hear this," Nick responded.

"The only thing you should be sorry about is that I didn't have the guts to turn in my own brother." Stephanie pulled a tissue from her skirt pocket.

"I don't know what to say to that, except it's too late now. At this point, we have to move forward." Nick touched the woman's arm and she leaned into him.

For someone who'd been molested as a child, I expected her to flinch at his touch. But what did I know? Maybe being molested made you crave attention from others.

"It is too late to fix the past, but I'm loath to help you find William's killer. You see, I want to wrap my arms around him and thank him for doing what I should have done years ago."

I kinda, sorta had to agree with Stephanie, in every way.

"I tried to warn Anna's mom about him, but he got to me first. William's secret was safe as long as I was terrified of him. Believe me, I was truly terrified. William hung and skinned my cat as a warning to me when he thought I was about to reveal his dirty secret. I've never had another pet, or a boyfriend."

Stephanie sniffed, and blew her nose into the tissue.

I concentrated on my breathing, afraid I'd start crying for the woman.

"I was more worried about what William would do if I told people about him, or turned him in, than I was about his other victims." She choked up a bit.

"They called Anna's mom yesterday. Since she's the next of kin, Bridget had to identify and sign for the body. Anna and Crissy have been here since then. Anna told me everything."

Now tears welled in my eyes. I looked at Nick for a reaction. I could see he was holding his breath.

"What did Anna tell you?"

"Oh God, she told me about her friends. She helped her dad find other girls, through her social networking pages, so he'd be satisfied, and leave her and her little sister alone."

My breath caught. Catey's best friend had set her up. Stunned, this time I stopped walking. When Nick looked back at me, I still didn't move. What the hell was wrong with these people?

After a moment of shock, I stopped judging. If William had scared his own sister so badly, what had he done to his daughter?

"When did Anna tell you about this?" Nick now had his arm around Stephanie's shoulder. He turned her around, and we started walking back toward the house.

Stephanie was visibly shaking, and her words came in short, erratic bursts. "Please, don't be mad at Anna. She's a little girl. She didn't want William to hurt her sister."

I couldn't take it anymore. "Where the hell was their mother during all of this?"

Nick shot me a piercing glance, and not the good kind.

"That's just it. I'm not sure what's wrong with these women that they are in such denial." Her breathing more normal, the tears had stopped. "I don't know how a woman doesn't see that her husband is more interested in touching his children than his wife."

"Look, this is water under the bridge. We need to know if William had any physical contact with Tiffany Anderson."

"Tiffany Anderson?"

I know it was Nick's question to answer, but I said, "She's allegedly one of William's victims, and she's gone missing. Since he's dead, we have no way of knowing if she's been kidnapped, run away, or if she's dead. We're at a loss."

"I'm trying so hard to keep Anna isolated from all of this. She's not even going to the funeral. She doesn't want to." Stephanie removed Nick's arm from her shoulder, now standing taller. "You can talk with Anna, but please, don't tell her that you know about what she did."

I wanted to break away and call Jackie so bad. I wanted to be mad at Anna, shake her, and scream, "Why did you do this to Catey?" But who was I to judge? I didn't grow up in the perfect family either.

When we approached the front door, Stephanie turned and said, "Wait here."

I could hear Stephanie calling Anna's name. "So, what do you think?"

Nick looked at me. I don't think I've ever seen him look so sad. "I think I wish I could call my mom and tell her thank you."

"Thank you for what?"

"Even though my dad wasn't a pedophile, he was abusive. The first time he laid a hand on me, other than for a proper spanking, he broke my arm."

I gasped. I had no idea Nick grew up in an abusive environment. "Oh, I'm so sorry."

"Don't be. My mom was the least selfish person I've ever known. She called the police, pressed charges, and then filed for divorce." He smiled at a distant memory.

"Strong woman." Now I knew where his personality came from.

"And when the restraining order didn't keep him away, she moved us. One day she packed everything we had and said she'd found us a new home."

"He never tried to find you?"

"Maybe he did. But this was in the days before the Internet, and I just don't think he found the time. It's not like my grandparents were going to tell him anything. They lived in South Africa."

I was learning more and more about Nick. "South Africa? Why didn't your mom move you there?"

"Because she was a US citizen, and she intended to never give that up, abusive husband or not." Nick laughed.

I wasn't sure what there was to laugh about, so I just smiled.

When Stephanie opened the door to usher us inside, Anna was standing next to her.

I don't know what I expected of Anna - tears, swollen eyes? She was the same height and weight as Catey, but she seemed frail. Her sienna hair was cut in a shoulder length bob, and looked like it had some sort of hair product, because its shine was unnatural. Her bluebell eyes were wide and clear. No signs of recent tears.

Stephanie made introductions all around, and then said, "They want to talk to you about Tiffany Anderson."

This was definitely a formality, since I was pretty sure these two women were thick as thieves, and Stephanie had briefed her before opening the door.

We followed them into the living room and Anna said, "What do you want to know?"

The room was over-decorated with tchotchkes on every surface, along with dust and cat hair. I wanted to wipe off the couch before I sat down because of all the cat hair, but I sat anyway. Nick hesitated, too.

"We need to know if Tiffany was one of Dylan's friends."

"Dylan?" Anna sucked at acting.

"I know you know your dad's alias was Dylan. And I'm pretty sure you were in on this whole thing from the beginning." Nick didn't pull any punches.

Anna sat, frozen.

Nick continued, "We have some pretty good computer forensics techs working for the police department, and we know you helped your dad meet these girls."

Anna leaned forward. "Not Tiffany. She wasn't his normal type."

"What was his type?" Nick asked.

Anna looked at me. "Catey."

I wanted to look away, but I stared at Anna, waiting.

"Tiffany wasn't really pretty enough, but she pursued him. She wanted me to introduce her to Dylan, because she said Catey wasn't good enough for him.

She said she'd be much better. I mean, we were all friends on that site. But Tiffany contacted Dylan, my dad, in other ways." Anna looked down to her lap and shook her head. "He said he only wanted to flirt with them, because they make him feel young again. He said that would be enough."

"Enough for what?" Nick gently probed.

Anna looked down at her hands. "Enough for him to leave my sister alone."

I just didn't understand. This man had custody rights?

"Anna, your parents are divorced?" I asked.

"No, they're just separated."

Nick stepped in. "And you and your sister would stay with your dad?"

"Sometimes. But mostly, Crissy would scream, cry, and beg not to have to go. Then Mom would give in, and Dad would be pissed." Anna smiled at the thought.

"Do you know if your dad ever had physical contact with Tiffany?"

Before Anna could answer, Nick got a phone call. "I'm sorry, I have to take this." He walked out of the room.

"Does Catey hate me?" Anna looked worried for the first time.

"Honey, Catey doesn't even know."

"Are you going to tell her?" Anna's eyes pleaded with me to say no.

"I think it's your place to tell her, not mine." And I hoped she'd be a good enough friend to 'fess up, or I'd be talking to Jackie about it soon enough.

"Absolutely. I tried to tell her before. I did everything I could to keep them from meeting." Now

Anna was biting her nails, which I hadn't noticed before, were already nubs.

"I know you did. Jackie and I had a talk with Catey. And I want to thank you for not letting it go too far. But, you see, it easily could have escalated if someone hadn't killed your dad."

Seeing the fear in Anna's eyes, I realized I shouldn't have mentioned William's murder.

"Someone had to stop him," Stephanie, who'd been quiet and still, interjected.

"It's not like he didn't deserve it," Anna said.

There was a loud bang as the front door opened and slammed shut. I looked, expecting to see that Nick had left.

A woman, who looked to be in her thirties burst into the room. She was an older version of Anna, apricot skin and sienna hair flowing down her back in loose curls. She was beautiful, a glimpse of what Anna would look like in twenty-plus years.

"Mom!" Anna jumped up.

"Bridget." Stephanie stood.

"How are the girls?" I noticed dark circles under her eyes.

"We're okay, Mom." Anna hugged her. "We're just talking to the police. Crissy is in Stepanie's office, playing video games."

She looked across to Nick. "Have they found his killer?"

I went to stand near Nick, who was now off the phone.

Nick approached the women. "We're still working on it."

Bridget stared him up and down. "And you are?"

Again, Nick flashed his badge and introduced himself.

"I just came from the morgue. I had to identify what's left of William." She looked at me. "I thought the woman I was with, Detective Mason, was your partner?"

"She is. This is a private detective. We're working on a missing person's case and thought Anna might be able to help us, since she knew the girl." Nick fidgeted with his phone, but didn't put it away.

Not really concerned, she asked, "Who?"

Anna said, "I don't think you know her mom. It's Tiffany Anderson."

"So you're a homicide detective. What are you doing to find my husband's murderer?" She seemed only slightly more concerned about Williams murder than she did the missing girl.

"Like I said, we're working on it." Exasperated, he said, "You're Anna's mother?"

A bit more resigned, she said, "I'm Bridget Garrison."

"Mrs. Garrison, where were you yesterday morning?"

Bridget's jaw dropped. "Did you really just ask me that?"

"Yes, ma'am, I did. He's your husband, and he was a predator, so I can see how you may not care for him much." Nick spoke as if Bridget was a small child.

"What does that have to do with where I was yesterday morning?" Bridget was indignant.

"It's just a question I have to ask Mrs. Garrison."

"Well, you can ask your partner. I've already spoken to her at length."

"Look Mrs. Garrison, your pedophile husband is dead, which is probably better for the world in general, but a girl is missing. She may be a victim of your husband's. Why won't you answer my question?"

Behind Bridget's back, Stephanie was shaking her head violently, seeming to silently scream, "No! Don't do this."

"I think it's time you leave." Bridget spat the words.

"Mrs. Garrison, I just got off the phone with my partner. She tells me you don't have an alibi for the time frame in which your husband was murdered. You do know what your husband was, don't you?"

"Get out. Get out now!" Bridget screamed.

Stephanie stepped in front of her sister-in-law. "This is my house, and as long as you're here, you may as well hear what the detective has to say."

Now Bridget turned on Stephanie. "No, I don't want to hear anything this stranger has to say. He doesn't know our family."

Bridget spun around toward the front door, only to find Anna standing in front of it. "Mom, please, for once just listen, because I've been too terrified to tell you all these years."

Bridget's face went slack.

CHAPTER 14

"Are you hungry?" Nick asked, as we got back in his car.

I was, but I was also tired of this case. As much as I enjoyed spending time with Nick, I needed a break. "Not really. You can just drop me off at home on your way."

Nick didn't respond, and was quiet for the rest of the drive.

I walked in my house, closed the door and leaned against it. What kind of world did we live in, where men preyed on young teenage girls? I wondered if most parents had any idea how dangerous the Internet could be. Then again, it's dangerous for adults, too. Being smart was the only way to protect yourself.

I didn't have the energy to prepare a meal, so grabbed a bottle from the fridge and poured myself a glass of wine. Hair of the dog, so to speak.

And speaking of dogs, I looked in the backyard, sipped my wine, and watched Lola as she slept peacefully in her doghouse. I wanted her life at the moment.

I thought about calling Charles to see if he was okay, but I really wanted to be removed from the case for at least a few hours.

Suddenly, my clothes felt dirty, so I went into the bedroom and changed into grey yoga pants, a snug sports bra, and a fitted black workout shirt. Workout clothes, they aren't just for working out anymore.

Walking back into the living room, I grabbed a novel I'd been reading and curled up in my favorite club chair with a blanket.

Several pages into the novel, I realized I hadn't comprehended anything I'd read. My mind kept wandering. Sebastian, and why he'd disconnected and not returned my call. Charles, and what had caused him to lose it at the Anderson house. Nick, and what the hell was going on between us.

With Charles, I knew better than to breach the subject of his tirade. When he was ready to talk, he would, but more than likely, he would never bring up the subject again. There were things in Charles' past that would stay there forever. I was good with that.

Nick, why did he have to keep showing up in my life? He seemed to care, but just how much, I didn't know. Was the ball in my court? Maybe I needed to be the aggressor and let him know I wanted to take things a step further. How could I when I didn't know the answer myself?

One thing I did know, Sebastian had approached me. Whether or not I wanted to pursue it was another matter. I wasn't going to let him off the hook that easy.

I put my novel on the table next to my chair and pulled out my cell phone. One deep breath to gather my nerve, then I dialed.

I couldn't believe it; he'd ignored my call. I know, because it only rang two times before going to voicemail. I hesitated for a split second, contemplated leaving a message, and then hung up. Fucker!

Why did I put myself out there like that? I should have just let it be. Now I felt like shit for calling, and being so stupid as to believe he was really interested.

I slammed my phone on the table and it rang.

"Sorry, I have a new phone and I accidentally hung up on the call instead of answering." Sebastian's voice was low and sexy.

Inside my ego was screaming, "Yes! He called back." On the outside I was playing it cool.

"No big deal. It's just that you left so abruptly last night." Did I sound cool, or desperate?

"Things are nuts at work, too. We just picked up a huge account, and I'll be leaving for Paris in the morning." He sounded apologetic.

"Oh." My sixth sense told me this was the kiss off. *I'll be out of town for the rest of your life, sorry.*

"Mimi, it's not like that. I'll only be gone a few weeks."

"Like what?" Lame. "I'm sure you'll love Paris."

"No, I hate Paris. I don't speak the language, and they hate that. I'm just lucky our company hires a translator for the trip."

I got ready to disconnect. "If you feel like it, and you don't find a French model to fall in love with, call me when you get home." I pulled the phone from my ear and was poised to push the little red "goodbye asshole" button when I heard a noise.

"MIMI?"

I put the phone back to my ear. "What?"

"We still have tonight, if I'm not rushing things."

My heart nearly burst. Yes! "Tell you what, you bring me Chinese, and we can rush things a bit."

I hung up the phone and sprinted to the bathroom. I looked in the mirror and saw dark circles under my eyes, dry lips and hair that looked like rats had nested there.

A quick once over, I dabbed on a bit of concealer for the circles, and some lip stain and a smidgen of gloss on my lips. A quick dusting of blusher on the cheeks made me look a bit fresher.

On closer look, I swear I had more wrinkles than I'd had that morning. Nothing I could do about that in such a short time, so I moved on to see what I could do with my hair.

Ever notice when things aren't going well in a girl's life, she tends to make major changes to her hair? I'd almost done the same a few weeks earlier. I thought about it again as I grabbed my long waves at about shoulder length and contemplated cutting it. Then I dropped the length of it and examined the roots. Lifting and sifting through my scalp, I decided I still had a few weeks before I needed a touch up. But this time, I planned to go to my stylist and redo my caramel highlights.

Messy hair seemed to be in, so I just did some finger styling and pulled it up in a high, loose ponytail.

I'd contemplated changing clothes, but I didn't want to look to anxious or interested. Besides, by the time I'd thought of it, I could hear knocking at the door, and it was a bit too late.

I rushed to the door, but stopped short and did one last check in the mirror before looking in the peephole. God help me, I think ancient karma was coming back to haunt me. It was Charles.

I stepped to the side of the door and waited. Maybe if I didn't answer, he'd go away. I should've known it was too soon for it to be Sebastian. Charles was dead set on ruining my sex life, whether he knew it or not.

Charles knocked again and I jumped. The man had ESP (extra snoopy perception), and he knew I was home.

"Mimi," he yelled. "Get off the damn toilet and answer the door."

Because I've known Charles for so long, this wouldn't normally embarrass me, but just after he yelled, I heard another voice.

"Charles, how ya doing?"

It was Sebastian, and now I had to answer the door. I cursed Charles silently and opened the door wide.

"I hope you washed your hands." Charles pushed past me into the house.

"I wasn't on the toilet." I turned to see Sebastian with the classic brown paper bag. He'd bought a lot of food.

I must have been staring at the bags with a weird expression because he said, "I wasn't sure what you like."

My soul smiled, and I'm pretty sure it came through on my face. I stood on my tiptoes and kissed him on the cheek. "I'm easy. I pretty much like everything when it comes to Chinese."

"Chinese? I'm starving." Charles came back to the door and grabbed the bag from Sebastian. "I'll grab plates."

Great, so much for rushing things. I ushered Sebastian into the living room and closed the door.

"Did you invite Charles, too?" He looked a bit disappointed.

I looked back toward the kitchen, watching Charles disappear. "Sorry, he just showed up. He's been known to do that at times."

"No problem. Maybe it's for the best. That way we can't start something we can't stop." He winked, and we headed into the kitchen too.

"Am I interrupting something?" Charles feigned innocence.

"Not at all. Mimi and I were just going to eat Chinese and talk about the French." Sebastian helped Charles take down plates and dish out the food. Five plates in all: peanut chicken, cashew chicken, General Tso's chicken, beef with broccoli, and pork fried rice. Charles put the huge helping of white rice in a bowl.

"Sticks or forks?" I reached into the silverware drawer. I heard sticks and forks, so I brought both to the table.

"So Sebastian, what brings you here?" Charles stuffed his mouth full of beef with broccoli while he waited for the answer.

"Mimi invited me. We were going to discuss my trip to France." Sebastian rivaled Charles in the stuff your mouth contest.

I picked at my delicious plate of cashew chicken and watched the two men. I figured when they were ready, they'd include me.

"I see." It sounded more like "I shee" as Charles was speaking around his food.

"You?" Even though Sebastian had food in his mouth too, it didn't sound as bad.

"I just brought something for Mimi to see. I thought she might find it was interesting." Charles stopped eating for a moment and pulled his iPad out of the messenger bag he'd brought in with him.

I was intrigued, but said, "You couldn't have called first?"

"It's not like you're ever doing anything." Charles glanced at Sebastian. "Well, it's not like this is normal."

I could have strangled him, but then the homicide unit would arrive and...oh my freaking God, there was another knock at the door.

I slammed my fork onto the table and went to go answer. I didn't even bother to look in the peephole before opening the door wide. Shit, I thought for sure it was going to be Jackie.

"Hello, Nick!" It just couldn't get any better than this - every man in my life in the same room at the same time. "Come on in, we're eating Chinese food."

Nick looked past me into the kitchen. "We?"

"Yeah, Charles and Sebastian are here, too."

"Sebastian's here? Charles called and said to meet here. He had something." Confusion clouded Nick's expression.

"Oh, the more the merrier. Come on in." I felt a pulsing headache coming on.

Nick and Sebastian were polite, but barely acknowledged each other.

Once we were seated and Nick's plate was full, Charles opened the cover on his iPad, and we all scooted close together to look. Since this wasn't classified, Sebastian looked, too.

"See that?" Charles pointed at a picture of someone's backyard.

"What are we looking at? It's someone's yard." Nick squinted and looked closer.

I saw it immediately. "It's the neighbor."

Charles pointed to the face just on the other side of the fence. "The neighbor was looking over the fence into William's yard when this photo was taken."

Everyone had stopped eating, except Sebastian. It's not like any of this interested him, and by now I'm sure he wanted the hell out of here.

Curious, I asked, "Do you know who took the photo?"

"I have no way of knowing, but it was on William's hard drive, along with hundreds of other family photos. Seems they had quite a few backyard picnics. There are at least a dozen BBQ photos. Some with only adults, but most had small children and tweens in them."

This picture had a slightly younger looking Anna along with four other young girls, all dressed in bathing suits and playing on a Slip-N-Slide™. The neighbor was only visible peering through the fence because Charles had enhanced the photo. I couldn't identify the other girls with Anna.

We were all silent for a moment, just staring and analyzing. I could hear Sebastian chewing. I looked up and smiled. He smiled back, a bit of sauce running down his lip. I reached across and wiped it.

Suddenly, it seemed all eyes were on me. I wiped my hand on a napkin, and diverted my attention back to the iPad photo.

"So maybe this neighbor knows something about the goings on at the Garrison house." Nick pulled a pad of paper from his pocket and flipped through the pages.

"Seriously, Nick? Paper? It is 2012." Charles was appalled that Nick didn't have some sort of digital device, just a pen and paper.

"Yes, Charles, because I know exactly how to use a pen and paper without needing hours of technical training, and I know where my notepad is at all times. It can never be hacked, and never be accidentally erased. Just ask my old homicide partner about that shit." He'd stopped flipping.

Charles coughed out, "Stone age."

"Here," Nick pointed to his pad. "The patrol officers canvassed the neighborhood asking questions, and no one seemed to know anything about William Garrison. They said he was quiet and kept to himself. I haven't heard back from anyone who seemed suspicious. As a matter of fact, everyone seemed shocked that this happened." He flipped the pad shut.

"So?" If Nick wasn't going back to William's neighborhood, I sure as hell was. "What now?"

We'd eaten at least half from each of the plates and most of the steamed rice when Nick stood. "So much for eating. Come on, Mimi, let's go."

I looked at Sebastian. I wouldn't be seeing him again for weeks. He looked at me with a weak smile. He knew he'd lost.

"Go," he waved me on. "I'll see you in a few weeks."

"Don't mind me," Charles mumbled, and shoved more rice in his mouth.

I hesitated. This was so rude. "I'll meet you out in the car. I need to change clothes and say goodbye to Sebastian."

I was pretty sure I saw the veins in Nick's tired eyes get even redder. "Make it quick, time is of the essence here," Nick said, and he was gone.

So said the man who'd just been sitting at my table stuffing his face full of Chinese food Sebastian had paid for.

"Charles, give Sebastian some money for the food we ate. I'm sure he wasn't expecting to be paying for dinner for four."

I leaned down and kissed Sebastian on the cheek. "I'm so sorry about this, but a teenage girl is missing."

"Some things just aren't meant to be, I guess." He put his hands around my neck and pulled me close. Then he kissed me on the forehead. In my ear he whispered, "So much for rushing things."

My heart thumped hard, and I took his hands and kissed them. "Have a safe trip. And if you get lonely, call me."

I left before I could do anything stupid. Instead of completely changing my clothes, I slipped on black ballet-style shoes and a long blazer to camouflage the yoga pants.

I heard Charles say, "You aren't really going to Paris, are you?"

I hummed to myself, so I couldn't hear Sebastian's response. As I walked out the front door of my house, I knew I'd never hear from him again. I wasn't sure if I was okay with it.

When I got in the passenger seat of Nick's car, he said, "Really, what's up with you two?"

I could honestly say, "Absolutely nothing. Just friends. He was coming over to say goodbye before he leaves for Paris."

Nick was silent, but I thought I saw a grin on his lips.

"So why am I going with you? You want me to work my feminine wiles on the neighbor?"

Nick flipped his notes open again and called in on his car radio. He asked the dispatcher for the homeowners' information for the houses on either side of the Garrison home. He gave the dispatcher house numbers, and he waited.

"No, I've seen you work your feminine whiles, and we aren't that desperate yet."

I smacked him on the shoulder just as the dispatcher came back on the radio. "2304 is Gretchen Miller, and 2300 is Leonard Crowhopper."

Nick disconnected. "Mr. Crowhopper must be our nosy neighbor. Let's pay him a visit."

Not that I was one to look a gift horse in the mouth, since there was no reason for Nick so let me be any part of this case, but I asked, "Why am I coming along?"

"So I can keep an eye on you." His matter-of-fact tone made me wonder what he was up to.

"Did I do something?"

"I don't know, but after I get the 411 on this Crowhopper guy, I'll have time to talk to you. And I want you where I can get in touch without having to track you down." He pulled the car over in front of Garrison's house.

I thought I saw the curtains move at Crowhopper's house, but it could've been my imagination.

Nick didn't get out of the car immediately, but when he did, he said, "Stay here a minute."

He went to the trunk of his car, came around and opened the passenger door. I noticed he had a black Kevlar vest and homicide jacket in his hands.

"We can't be too careful. Put these on." He handed me the vest first.

I got out of the car and put the vest on, adjusting it to fit snugly. Nick turned me around and made a few more adjustments. After a few more tugs and pulls, he helped me put on the Salinas Police Department jacket. It was a little big, but covered the vest nicely. The ballet slippers were a bit out of place, but how did I know I'd be playing pretend cop?

"Ready?" Nick asked.

"Do you think this is really necessary?" I shoved my hands in the pockets.

"Just play along for a change." Nick walked in front of me toward Crowhopper's house.

We both stood to the side of the front door. Nick knocked and we waited. And waited. He knocked again. "Mr. Crowhopper? Salinas Police Department. Please answer the door."

I was sure I could hear some noise inside, but no one answered the door. I looked at Nick. "Well?"

"Let's just wait another minute." He knocked again.

Finally, a voice said, "Just a minute. I'm coming. Please don't knock down my door."

Nick stepped back. I had to admit, the man's voice didn't sound very intimidating. We looked at each other, and then both turned to the door when we heard the lock move.

"Leonard Crowhopper?" Nick asked when the man opened the door wide.

"Yes? What can I do for you?"

I'd seen him before. He was the neighbor who came out to talk to Charles and me. He wasn't at all meek then, and didn't seem meek now. I wondered why he'd been hesitant to open his door.

"Is there a reason you didn't open the door immediately?" Nick flashed his badge.

Leonard looked at his feet, turned crimson, then looked at Nick, but not in the eye. "Bad timing?"

How ironic.

Nick looked skeptical. "Do you mind if we come in?"

"No," Leonard opened the door fully. "Sorry, I've been working and the place is a bit untidy."

I stepped into the house and Nick followed. I only wish my house was this untidy.

The décor was simple, like a bachelor in an apartment. According to the records Mr. Crowhopper owned this house, but it barely looked lived in. There was a sofa, loveseat, and a chair, all of black fabric, centered around a simple glass topped coffee table. No art on the walls, no throw pillows, not even a magazine. I could see why he apologized for the mess, as there was a microwave dinner on the coffee table, along with a glass of milk and a plate of brownies.

"What do you do for a living, Mr. Crowhopper?" Nick asked, as he took in the sparse décor.

"I work for an Internet security company." He sounded proud. "Please, my name is Leonard."

"Thanks, Leonard. I'm Nick Christianson, and this is Mimi Capurro."

Leonard took a better look at me. "Oh, hi, we met…well, you know when."

"Do you drive all the way to the Silicon Valley for work every day?"

"Not anymore. I telecommute, which is much easier and a lot less expensive with the price of gas these days." Leonard waved us into the living room. "Please, sit."

We both sat on the loveseat - how quaint.

"What exactly do you do for this Internet security company?" Nick sat at the edge of the seat, looking ready to bolt at any moment.

"I find holes." He waved his hands in the air. "I find back doors, security leaks, holes in the system, then I sell the companies a patch."

"So you're a hacker?" That's what it sounded like to me.

"Oh no, I have permission to look. Major companies hire our company to find the security weaknesses. So yes, I'm a hacker, but I have permission."

"So being nosy is your business," Nick stated.

"I guess so." Leonard grinned at this.

"And maybe you're nosy about more than just computer security?"

Leonard crossed his arms over his chest. "Meaning?"

"I have a picture or two of you peeking into your neighbor's backyard during his get-togethers." Nick handed him a copy of one of the pictures Charles had provided.

Leonard looked at the photo carefully. "Where did you get this?"

"From William's computer."

"And did you see what else is on that man's computer?" Leonard uncrossed his arms and leaned forward.

"You've seen William's computer?"

"Fine, I'll admit it, I'm nosy. I'm not sure William should be having any BBQ parties with young girls in his backyard."

Now Nick was mirroring Leonard and leaning in. "So you *have* seen what's on the computer?"

"Why don't you ask his sister?" Leonard avoided looking at Nick. He played with the brownie on the plate.

"I'm asking you."

"I may have gotten a glimpse, but I haven't *looked* at it. That would be an invasion of privacy." Leonard picked at the crumbs on the plate. "Talk to the sister."

"What does William's sister know?" I asked, wanting to slap his hand away from the brownies.

"I'm not sure how she knows, but it's like radar. Every time there're young girls at William's house, she shows up. And not long afterward, the girls leave. When his daughters visit, she's there the whole time."

This was news.

Nick seemed intrigued. "Just how often do you watch what's happening next door?"

Leonard laughed, warily. "I work from home. I'm single, and I get bored very easily. Most of my hacking is done at night. In the daytime, I snoop. Not anything illegal, like with cameras or telescopes, but I look and listen."

"Were you listening the day William Garrison was killed?"

"I was not." Leonard gave Nick his full attention. "But I did see William's sister arrive at the house that morning. I'm not sure if William had left for work yet, as he usually parks his car in the garage, but I didn't see him leave."

"Did you see or hear anything?" Nick leaned his elbows on his knees as he listened.

"I did not." Leonard thought a moment. "Well, there was the slamming door."

"What door?"

"It sounded like the front door."

"Who was it?"

"I'm just not sure. I was, um, indisposed when I heard it. It was quite a disturbing interruption."

I smiled.

Nick grinned. "I'm sure it was. Could it have been William's sister?"

"Could've been. She was the only person I saw at the house that day."

I was sure he was lying. What about when Jackie was there? And when Charles and I were snooping about?

"Really?" Nick sounded like he thought the man was lying, too.

"I'd gone to the store right after I went to the bathroom. And I'd just gotten home when the police had swarmed the neighborhood. You can ask the patrol officers who came to question me that afternoon."

"So you just happened to miss the biggest thing to happen in your neighborhood?" I just couldn't keep quiet any longer.

Leonard looked at me. "I know. Dumb luck." Then he considered. "If you want to know anything about that killing, I suggest you talk to William's sister.

She was on him like white on rice, and not in a loving way. I think she was really mad at him for something."

Nick stood. "Here's my card. If you think of anything, please call me."

"Thanks, but I just don't have anything to tell. Damn, something this juicy and I miss out. After all the years I've been watching William, I miss out."

Nick and I headed to the front door.

"Mind if I ask you a question?" Leonard sounded sheepish.

"Well, you've answered all of mine," Nick said.

"If it was the sister who killed William, and she was protecting someone, would it be considered self-defense?"

"That's for the courts to decide."

I asked a question I wondered why Nick didn't ask. "Have you ever seen any young girls, say fourteen or fifteen, go into William's house?"

Leonard perked up. "Sure, all the time. He had daughters, you know."

Nick asked, "Other than his daughters?"

I wondered why Nick didn't describe Tiffany.

"I guess. I mean his daughters had friends." Leonard led us to the door.

"What about when the daughters weren't around?"

Leonard opened the door, nearly rushing us out. He contemplated a moment. "Probably. Maybe. Could be."

"Is that a yes, Leonard?" Nick's impatience getting the better of him.

"I'd have to say, maybe, yes."

"Do you have a number where I can reach you?"

"Sure, why?" He reached in his pocket and handed Nick a business card. "The second one is my cell number."

"I may have a few more questions, but I don't want to bother you anymore tonight."

"No bother," Leonard said, as he shut the door.

CHAPTER 15

"Now what?" I asked. "Do you think Stephanie killed William?"

"I wouldn't blame her. But I don't think Leonard is telling us all he knows." Nick said as he flipped open his notepad.

"Well, she did say she should have. Maybe she did."

"I'm not sure she looks like a murderer." He scribbled something down. "Not that a murderer has a look."

Just then, my phone rang. I looked at the caller I.D. and held my finger up for Nick to wait. "Give me just a sec. I need to answer this."

He pointed to the car and headed that way. I stayed on the sidewalk.

"What's up?" I asked.

"That's what I was going to ask you." Charles sounded harried.

"We just left Leonard Crowhopper's house. Something doesn't seem right about him. I feel like he's hiding something." I kept my voice down, so Nick couldn't hear.

"You think he killed Garrison?" I could almost feel Charles's radar beeping.

"Not that so much, but that he knows something he's not telling us." Then I got an idea.

"You want me to keep an eye on his place tonight?" Charles took the words right out of my mouth.

"Have I told you lately how much you scare me?"

"I'll be there in ten minutes." Charles hung up.

I assumed he and Sebastian had finished eating, and that my vampire boy was gone, because Charles would never leave him in my house alone.

I walked back to the car, and saw Nick staring intently at me. I quietly took off the police jacket and vest, and got into the passenger seat.

"What was that all about?" He tried to act nonchalant.

"It was Charles being nosy. He's coming over to keep an eye on Leonard. I just thought maybe it was best not to let him out of sight for too long." I settled in and buckled my seatbelt.

"Something really did strike you about that guy, didn't it?" Nick drove away from Leonard's house.

"I don't know what it was, but I'll bet he's nosier and knows more than he's letting on."

"Uh-huh," Nick mumbled. "Still hungry?"

"Sure."

I expected we'd zoom through one of the myriad of drive thru restaurants in town, but Nick drove toward the community college. There weren't any quick service restaurants in this area, but there was a coffee shop and a bagel place. Even more surprising, he turned down a residential street. I can't tell you the name, to protect his privacy, but I'll tell you the driveway he pulled into was in front of a quaint little beige cottage.

"New restaurant in town?" I couldn't help myself.

Nick parked in front of the detached two-car garage. "My house."

I suppressed a smile, but my heart was beaming. I couldn't believe I was going to see the inside of Nick Christianson's house. I felt like we were in college again, and he'd invited me back to the frat house. And in reality, frat house was what I expected when I walked inside. Nick was never known for his housekeeping skills.

Nick opened a gate in the side yard, next to the garage, and held it until I walked through. I was treated to a landscape architect's wet dream. Under my feet were two by two cement pavers stained in various colors of brown and gray, and beyond the pavers, a geometric pattern of smaller pavers amongst pea rock.

I could see six raised gardens evenly dividing the rocks, and a line of neatly trimmed evergreens along the fence line. And just when I thought I couldn't be more amazed, I saw a several rows of garden vegetables planted along one of the walls of the house. The bottom row looked like herbs, with the next row resembling onions or chives, and the top row was butter, red leaf and green leaf lettuce. I stood in awe.

Nick walked right by me and unlocked the back door. "You coming?"

"Not yet…"and I meant that in so many ways.

He left me standing there and went into the house.

When I got over my shock of seeing his immaculate yard, and homegrown veggies, I went inside.

Let me just say, he'd come a long way since his college days.

--

The door he'd opened led into a small galley kitchen. There wasn't even a toaster on the counter, much less dishes in the sink. The kitchen had honey oak cabinets with textured glass windows, flesh colored granite countertops and backsplash. The stainless steel appliances made the space scream bachelor pad. I was suddenly ashamed I'd ever let Nick in my less than tidy house.

Before I knew it, Nick had left the room and come back wearing shorts and a v-neck white t-shirt. Kitchen, what kitchen? At that moment all I could see were Nick's broad shoulders and the way his tawny biceps filled out his shirt.

"Make yourself at home." He pointed toward the next room. "I'm going to grab some lettuce and herbs from the garden and make us a couple of salads. Do you like salmon?"

I think I was still mesmerized by his torso because I just nodded. I went to the dining room to sit on one of the bar stools that lined the breakfast bar along the wall. This room was light and airy, and the décor complimented the kitchen. Masculine, but something any woman would love to have in her home.

When Nick came back in, I'd come to my senses and asked, "Can I help with anything?"

"Yeah, over in the corner there is a wine fridge. Grab the bottle of Louis Roederer Cristal Brut."

He said this as if I was grabbing an ordinary bottle of sparkling wine.

"Champagne?" He had to be kidding.

"Why not? I think it'll be great with the salads." Nick had already begun chopping and slicing.

"Can we say overkill?" I was sure he was showing off because of the package Sebastian had sent.

"Mimi, really, stop over-analyzing and open the damn bottle."

Fine. I mean, who was I to turn down a nice bottle of champagne? I went over to the wine refrigerator and found the bottle. Only it wasn't just one bottle, he had five. And I won't even bore you with the other labels I spied while I snooped.

Under my breath, I said, "Who knew?"

"Huh?" He brought the plates over to the dining room table.

"I thought you didn't drink." This made no sense to me.

"I don't." He placed a bottle of San Pellegrino in front of one plate, and an empty (chilled, I might add) flute in front of the other plate.

"I'm not going to drink alone. I'll have Pellegrino, too."

Nick surprised me again by leaning over and kissing me on the forehead. "It's not well known that I'm in recovery, so people give me expensive wine all the time. Someone has to enjoy it."

Just then something possessed me, and I was done playing games. I didn't want the damn champagne. I didn't want the stupid salad. I wanted Nick.

"I'm not really hungry or thirsty," I said. And the next thing I know, I took a leap of faith, stood on my tiptoes and kissed Nick on the mouth.

Nick pushed me away. "What about Sebastian?"

My phone vibrated with a text message. I had to check it.

"What about him? Let me rephrase that: The ball is in your court. It's either you or Sebastian, but you have to tell me right this moment."

"Why is that?" Nick took another step away from me.

"Because this is a text message from him." I shoved my phone at Nick.

He pushed it back to me without looking at it. "Look Mimi, I have things…"

I rolled my eyes. He always had "things."

"Hear me out." He stepped closer and grabbed my hands. "I don't know what I have to offer anyone, but I'm willing to offer you one day at a time. If that's good enough for you, then we can see where this goes. If it's not, then I'll put these salads in the refrigerator, and give you a ride to wherever you want to go."

I looked at the phone, then at Nick. His piercing blue-gray eyes melted me, just like an iceberg in global warming. I put the phone away, grabbed the salad plates and the Pellegrino, and put them in the fridge. Then I took Nick by the hand and navigated my way toward his bedroom.

I heard him say, "Are you sure about this?"

It'd been way too long for me to question whether or not I was sure about anything. I just knew I needed to have sex, and Nick seemed like a good candidate.

I'm pretty sure we hadn't been in the bedroom for a full minute when I heard a familiar sound.

"You have got to be freaking kidding me!" I was nearly shouting.

"Just answer it." Nick rolled over onto his back.

My cell phone rang, then Nick's, then mine again. I reached over to the nightstand and grabbed my phone. "What!"

"Are you with Nick?" It was Charles.

"Why?" I was irritated and I didn't care who knew.

"Oh, no. Oh, shit. This is really bad timing, isn't it?"

The words were sincere enough, but the chuckle in his voice didn't sound like he cared that he was interrupting.

"What is it, Charles?" I nearly spat the words.

"You're going to kill me, but I need you to come right now." The chuckle was gone.

I sat straight up. "What's going on?"

"You said to keep an eye on Leonard. Well, I followed him when he left his house. You are never going to believe where he went."

"Where?" I was already out of bed and putting my shoes on. Yes, just my shoes.

"To some barn, I think it belongs to Stephanie." The name hung in the air.

"Are you there now?" I asked Charles. Then to Nick I said, "We've gotta go."

Nick was out of bed, dressed, and pulling on his shoulder holster. He grabbed his keys and I kept talking to Charles as we headed out to the car.

"Not anymore. I'll text you the address so you can put it in Nick's navigation system."

Charles disconnected, and I had a text a moment later. I looked at it, then at Nick. "Prunedale?"

CHAPTER 16

If you've never been in a cop car with the lights and siren on, cruising along at 110 miles per hour, I'm here to tell you, it's a rush. It's also scary as hell, but I just white knuckled it with my seatbelt firmly in place, and prayed like I've never prayed in my life. "Dear God, please let Nick know what the hell he's doing and not get us in a wreck." Not sure He was listening, but we did make the turn off at San Miguel Canyon Road in record time with a clear path in front of us.

Nick turned off the lights and siren when we turned off San Miguel Canyon Road to a small street. He slowed to a crawl as we looked for Charles' car. Even though we hadn't reached the address sent in his text, I saw his car parked on the shoulder of the road. Knowing how much Charles loves his car, I knew this had to be important, because it had to be life or death for him to leave the Spyder on the shoulder.

Nick had called his partner before we left town, telling her to meet us. Piper was a faster driver than Nick, because her car was parked in front of Charles'.

Nick pulled in behind the Spyder, and we both got out. I pulled out my cell and called Charles.

"We're here. Where are you?" I whispered, though I'm not sure why.

"Walk up two houses, then look in the row of bushes. Piper and I are hiding, watching the barn,"

Charles whispered. "And for goodness sake, be quiet. We don't want you announcing your arrival."

I disconnected and stuck my tongue out at the phone. I motioned for Nick to follow me, and we walked along the gravel shoulder for about 500 feet. When we got past the two houses, I realized I had no idea which side of the street Charles would be on. Nick pointed. It was the mailbox for the address Charles had provided. I looked to my left and saw just a barn.

It was an older style wood barn that looked like it had been refurbished. There was perfectly manicured lawn around it, with a gravel driveway that led to a walk-in door. The huge double doors of the barn creaked with the wind, but looked to be only decorative.

Nick headed into the row of bushes and I followed. We crouched down low and sidled up next to Charles.

"This better be good," Nick said. "You have no idea what I'm giving up to be here."

Charles winked. "Oh, I think I do."

I blushed.

Charles pointed. "She was already here when he arrived, but both Leonard and Stephanie were in there."

"I don't see any cars." I started to stand and take a closer look, but Charles yanked me down.

"Stephanie left already. Leonard's car is parked around the back. I've been around the perimeter, but I didn't want the neighbors calling the cops until you were here to vouch for me."

"You wanted me to vouch for your voyeurism?" Nick spoke to Charles, but his eyes never left the barn. "How long ago did Stephanie leave?"

Piper put her hand on Charles's shoulder. "I'll vouch for you."

Charles nudged her and she nearly toppled over. Their chemistry was cute.

"Five minutes or so." Charles answered. "I haven't seen any activity. No lights, but then it's still fairly light out, so maybe I just don't see them."

I stayed crouched, but I left the bushes. Nick tried to grab me, but I was out of his reach.

I stayed low and approached the mailbox. What the heck, I'd just see who this property belonged to. I looked around for oncoming traffic on the deserted street, saw no one, so I stood and opened the box.

There was only one piece in the box, addressed to *It's Soy Good Candle Company*. I put the letter back in the box and scooted back to the bushes.

"It's a candle company." Proud to offer up the tidbit.

"I know. I ran the address before we got here." Nick said.

My bubble properly deflated, I let my knees rest on the dirt and leaves.

"Now that you're here, I'm going down there to snoop a little," Charles stood tall.

Nick said, "Why did you wait for us if you'd planned to go in all along?"

"Because if he shoots me, or I shoot him, I need witnesses, and someone to call the ambulance." Charles didn't even go back to the road. He just approached the building from the bushes.

As Charles hiked down to the barn, I saw Leonard get in his car and drive away. He must not have seen Charles because he didn't stop, and he wasn't looking around as he drove out the driveway.

"I told you there was more to him than he let on."

"I just wonder exactly how well he knew Stephanie before all of this stuff happened with Garrison." Nick reached up and scratched the back of his head.

I scratched mine, too, but because it itched. Then the thought of ticks came to mind and I scrambled out of the bushes, toward the barn. I swear I could feel things crawling on me. Gross.

"Mimi, no." Nick whisper-yelled behind me.

As usual, I didn't listen. I followed Charles right down to the barn. Within seconds, I could hear Nick following behind me.

"I won't be an accessory to trespassing or breaking and entering. Stop," Piper said, then she came down behind Nick anyway.

I kept walking. When I got around to the other side of the barn, I saw Charles looking in a window. "See anything interesting?"

Charles looked disappointed. "It looks like a candle making facility." He pointed back to the window. "I like their label."

I didn't bother looking. "What now?"

Nick had caught up. "What now? I'll tell you what, you two are leaving. I'm not going to be the one to explain this to the cops, and believe me, I'm sure the neighbors are suspicious by now."

A voice came from the driveway. "We sure are."

A bulky woman of about fifty, wearing a housedress in a faded paisley print marched down toward us. She held a twelve-gauge shotgun across her chest. "Who the hell are you, and what are you doing on my property?"

Nick reached down to pull out his badge, and the woman leveled the shotgun at him. He put both hands up. "Hold up there, ma'am. I'm just getting out my identification. I'm with the Salinas Police Department."

She lowered her weapon. "Fine. But, just like they say in the movies, slowly."

Slowly, Nick pulled out his badge. He held it at arm's length for her to see, even though it was way too far away for her to tell what it said. "I'm investigating a homicide, ma'am."

"Homicide? You smell any dead bodies around here?" She had dropped the shotgun to her side and continued down the driveway toward us. "You best not be snooping on my private property without a warrant. I know my rights."

"I have reason to believe someone we've questioned in our investigation has something to hide here."

"You believe, huh? And who are these yahoos with you?" She used the shotgun as her pointer, when she indicated Charles, Piper and me.

Nick took a minute before responding. "My partner and some people I work with." Without explaining further he asked her, "Do you own this barn?"

"I own the property, but it's leased to It's Just Soy Good. What's it to you?"

Nick ignored her question. "You know Leonard Crowhopper?"

The woman laughed. "What the hell kind of name is that?"

"So you don't know him?" Nick's frustration was evident in his tone.

"I don't know. Maybe I do, maybe I don't. So who's dead?"

"Right now, we're looking for a missing girl. We've already found the dead person." Piper pulled out a picture of Tiffany. She stretched her arm out, but didn't approach the woman.

The woman approached Piper as if she were a rattle snake and took the photo from her hand. "This the missing girl, or the dead body?"

"Missing girl."

In all of this exchange, I was surprised by how quiet Charles and I were being. We've never been known to let someone else take the lead, but that shotgun had us firmly in place with zipped lips.

"Huh, never seen her." She handed the picture back.

"Do you have a key to this barn?" Nick sounded a bit friendlier.

"Nope," she shook her head. "What would you be wantin' in there for?"

"This Leonard person my partner asked about, he was here earlier. I was just wondering what interest he had in this barn." Piper carefully pocketed Tiffany's picture.

"Don't know no Leonard. A Stephanie Garrison is the president of the candle company, maybe he's a friend of hers, or an employee." The woman's body language had relaxed a bit.

Nick reached in his pocket and pulled out a business card. "Ma'am, I'm Homicide Detective Nick Christianson. Please take this card. And if you see anything suspicious, please call me right away."

She snatched the card and tucked it in between her breasts. She said, "Irma Tucker."

"Nice meeting you. We'll be on our way, Mrs. Tucker. Please, if you see anything, call me, and I'll come right back."

"Like I said, I ain't seen no suspicious activity. Sometimes that Stephanie woman is out here at odd hours, but that ain't nothing. Being self-employed means you don't get no regular nine to five."

"True," I said.

Irma's chubby neck nearly snapped when she turned to look at me. It was as if she just realized I was standing there. I knew better, but I wasn't sure as I watched her gape at me.

"I'm sorry, it's just that I'm self-employed, too. Crazy hours we keep." I gave a self-deprecating smile.

"You should be at home making babies. Where is your man that he doesn't provide for you?" She snapped.

I contemplated the answer to that, and then said, "Ma'am, he's dead."

Her face softened. "What?"

Nick and Charles now looked at me the way Irma had been. Charles looked to Nick, as if indicating maybe he was my man.

Well, he was wrong. Nick wasn't my man. Dominic had been my man, and he was dead. Nick might be my new partner in fun, but he definitely was not my man. Yet.

Irma said, "Just how many men do you have, sweetie? 'Cuz these boys look a bit confused."

"None. My husband died a few years ago. It's just me now." I looked down and scuffed the dirt with my foot.

Changing the subject, Nick said, "So you don't have a key to this barn?"

"Not without a warrant, I don't." She hiked the shotgun over her shoulder. "But I promise, if I see anything suspicious, or I see the precious girl you showed me, I'll call."

With that, she turned and headed up the drive.

We all started to converge when she turned back around and yelled, "Now get the hell off my property before I call the cops. You're trespassing."

She waited at the road to be sure we left. As I walked by her, I handed her my business card.

"A P.I., huh?" Irma tucked the business card in with Nick's, and laughed. "More liked P.I.T.A."

CHAPTER 17

Nick decided he needed to get back to the police station and find out a little more about Stephanie Garrison, so I got a ride home with Charles.

Once again, my day hadn't gone as planned. I wanted to call Jackie and see if she'd found out anything from talking to Catey, but I knew if she had something to share, she'd call me.

I hadn't spent nearly enough time with Lola over the last few days, so I decided to make some popcorn and spend the evening in. I'd never gotten around to finishing Lauren Silke's novel, *Prey*, so I took the bowl of popcorn into the living room, curled up on the corner of the couch and started reading.

It wasn't long before Lola climbed up next to me, stuffed bear in her mouth, and lay down. As hard as I tried to concentrate on the novel, the events of the week kept running through my head. This was apparently not my day for a relaxing read, either.

William and Stephanie had a tumultuous relationship because of his ways. I couldn't bring myself to even think the words for what he was. Stephanie visited William often enough that Leonard knew her. Or did Leonard know her in some other way?

Why is it that families are in such denial about their relatives? Did Anna's mom really have no idea about William? And what the hell was wrong with Stephanie that she didn't stop them from getting married and having kids? I'd never understand family dynamics, but this one really baffled me.

I held the book open in my lap, but I kept finding myself staring off into space. There had to be something I could do on my own. Something I could do that wouldn't be breaking the law, or endanger the investigation. I looked down at the words on the page again, and this time I saw Tiffany's face.

She was alive. I felt it in my bones. That girl was still alive. Terrified, and probably alone, but I could feel her breathing. Maybe she'd been the victim at the time of William's demise. Someone had saved that girl. A teenage girl could never have inflicted that much damage on a man, no matter how enraged.

I knew Stephanie had been keeping a closer eye on William than she'd admitted. Or maybe Anna had seen the relationship with Tiffany and her father go too far. What was Anna capable of doing?

I picked up my cell phone and used Switchboard to search Stephanie Garrison's name. Nothing. Shit. Then I searched the name of her business. Bingo, two numbers. I could just hope one of the numbers was her cell phone.

I started to dial the number, then disconnected. I pushed Lola off my feet and said, "Wanna play?"

I loaded Lola up in the car and took her to Tiffany's parents' house with me. I looked at my watch. Not too late. I could justify my arrival at such a late hour.

I braced myself and knocked on the door.

Julie answered, looked at me, and immediately slammed the door in my face. I guess I should've expected this reaction after the things Charles said.

I knocked again, harder. "Mrs. Anderson, please. I'm alone."

She opened the door again, but just a crack. "Are you here to insult my family again?"

"Hey, I didn't insult anyone. I was just along for the ride." I raised my hands in surrender. When I saw her start to close the door again, I said, "I think I may be able to find Tiffany."

She looked wary, but opened the door a bit wider. "What can you do that the police can't do?"

I turned and pointed to my car. I had the passenger window down, and half of Lola's body was hanging out the door. She wanted to get out in a big, bad way, but she had just enough discipline not to jump out of the car.

"Lola used to be a tracker. Not a professional, mind you, but I trained her for possible use at my detective agency."

"So?" She wasn't having any of it.

"I was hoping I could borrow a piece of clothing that belonged to your daughter to see if Lola's skills are up to par." It was worth a shot.

"The police dog didn't find anything." Julie Anderson started sniffling.

"I know the police have worked very hard on this case, but I'm not limited by the laws they are, and I have an idea."

"What's your idea?" Julie relented and let me in the door.

Within minutes, I had Tiffany's dirty skirt from the laundry, and was on my way to Leonard

Crowhopper's house. I just knew that girl had been there. But, if I was right, what was I going to do about it?

On the ride over, I let Lola play with the dirty skirt. She sniffed and tossed it in the air, and then she curled up on the seat with it tucked between her front legs.

When I arrived at Leonard's, I took the skirt from Lola, put it to her nose and said, "Suchen."

I put the skirt in the backseat, snapped a leash on Lola, and took her to Leonard's front door. Lola was a spoiled brat, but once on the leash, she was all business. She walked calmly beside me, with her ears erect.

I knocked, and waited. Leonard didn't take nearly as long to answer the door this time. Only, he opened it without unlatching his inside security chain. I wanted to tell him that chain wasn't any good because I could kick that door open before he knew what hit him, and Lola would be standing on his chest with her canines bared.

"What do you want now?"

"Mr. Crowhopper, that isn't a very nice way to greet someone who is trying to find a missing person," I said politely.

"I thought you were trying to find a killer." He snapped.

"Well, that too. But for now I'm looking for Tiffany Anderson. And I think you can help."

"I told you…"

I cut him off. "Lola, suchen."

Lola can track from about 100 feet if there isn't too much wind. She stood quietly. This wasn't a good sign.

"Mr. Crowhopper, please, I feel awkward talking to you through that chained door." I pointed to Lola and she sat.

"Too bad. I have nothing to say to you." He closed the door.

Okay, that went well. I stood there for a moment, contemplating my next move. I was sure Lola would sense that girl in Leonard's house. I didn't think the small crack in the door was a deterrent, as Lola could smell her target through a crack in the cement. Maybe I was wrong. Maybe Leonard Crowhopper was just a nosy neighbor and nothing more.

I gathered up Lola's leash and turned when I heard the door open behind me. "I'm sorry, I don't remember your name."

"Mimi," I said, but didn't turn back around. I decided I was finished here and started back to the car.

"Mimi, can I ask you a question?"

Now I turned around.

Leonard was standing in the doorway with the door fully open now. I took the opportunity to walk Lola back to the house. Leonard stepped back, but didn't close the door.

"Yes?" I prompted.

"Whoever killed William Garrison, do you think there is a possibility, if they were discovered, that they would face murder charges?"

"You asked this before. I don't know. It could have been self-defense. I wasn't there when he was killed, so I don't know what happened. Maybe."

"What do you mean maybe?" He wasn't just curious; he was desperate for an answer.

"Mr. Crowhopper, I believe the person who killed Mr. Garrison saved the world from a sadistic predator, so I'm hardly the one to give you an answer. I would say there's a great case for self-defense. Maybe not *self* defense, but defense of some kind." I paused. "Why, Leonard? What do you know?"

And that's when it happened. Lola dropped in place and crossed her front paws. It was barely audible, but I heard her whimper. I looked down. It was a positive. I let go of her leash and said, "Gutes Madchen, get ins Bett."

Lola made a beeline for the car, jumped in through the open passenger window, and went straight into the backseat. Within seconds, she had Tiffany's skirt in her mouth.

"What the hell was that?" Leonard stepped onto the porch. When he saw what Lola had in her mouth, he went pale.

"Leonard, Lola used to be a tracker. Not a professional, but a tracker all the same. What she has in her mouth is Tiffany's skirt."

"What are you trying to say?" He was back in the house and ready to slam the door shut again.

"I'm saying Tiffany Anderson has been here." I put my foot in the door to keep him from getting out of my sight.

"Leave me alone." He shoved the door hard, and it hurt like hell as he smashed my foot.

"Please, I'm not the cops. I just want to know that Tiffany is safe. I need to know that William Garrison didn't do anything to that poor girl." I shoved hard at the door. "Please, Leonard, talk to me."

That's when I saw the gun in his hand, and it was pointed directly in my face. I'm pretty sure it was a .44 Magnum, but at such close range, it was a bit blurry.

The blood was pumping through my veins so hard, I thought my heart was going to crack my ribs. Suddenly, Lola was out of the car and charging the house.

"Lola, no!" I yelled as he turned his gun from me to my dog.

"Ma'am, I think it's best you get your fucking foot out of my doorway." His color had returned with a vengeance.

With my heart still slamming against my ribs, and my breath in short supply, I pulled my foot back and the door slammed shut.

As I stood in place, trying to gather myself, I heard him say through the door, "I can't help you."

The first thought in my head at that moment should have been: *Wow, that was really stupid to approach a perfect stranger with an accusation like that*. Only before I had time to process the thought, my cell phone rang.

I looked at the number on the screen, Salinas area code, but I didn't recognize it. I started to hit the ignore icon, but changed my mind at the last second, and answered before it went to my voice mail.

"Ms. Capurro, it's Irma." Her voice didn't sound as steady and sure as it did in person. I wondered if it was the phone line.

"Irma, what can I do for you?" I tried to sound pleasant and not startled by the call. What could this woman possibly want from me?

"I think you should come see this." The shakiness was more pronounced.

"What's going on, Irma? I'm in the middle of a case at the moment." I just wanted to go home. My idea of using Lola was a mistake. Going out alone was a mistake. I wanted to go home, take a bath, and forget my mistakes for the day.

"I think you need to come by the candle place. There is something going on in that barn."

My breath caught. "Did you call Detective Christianson?"

"No. To be honest, he scares me a little."

"You didn't seem too intimidated by him earlier."

A nervous laugh. "A twelve-gauge shotgun does wonders for bravery."

I had to laugh. "You really should be calling the detective. I'm not the police."

The entire time I was telling Irma to call the cops, I was getting in my car. I made sure Lola was comfy, and then I flipped a u-turn and headed toward Prunedale. I only wished I could put a light on my roof, and drive at warp speed with lights and siren blazing.

"Irma, are you at home?" I put my cell phone in its cradle and put it on speaker.

"I'm at the end of my driveway. There is lots of activity in that barn, Ms. Capurro. Someone needs to get here now."

"I'm going to hang up and make a few phone calls. I want to you go back into your house and stay there. It may not be safe." I waited a moment, but there was no response. "Irma?"

The phone was dead. Shit! I pressed my speed dial for Charles.

Before he said anything, I said, "Meet me back at the barn."

"That candle place?" Charles perked up.

"That old lady called me from the number on my business card. She said something very interesting was going on, and that I should get there now."

"Did she call the cops?"

"No. I'm calling Nick next. I just wanted you to know first, so Nick couldn't say to stay out of it."

"Call him right now. We don't need to do anything to put Tiffany in more danger than she may already be in. I don't want that on my conscience." Charles disconnected without saying goodbye.

It took every ounce of power to keep from flooring the accelerator. I had to stay cool. I dialed Nick's phone.

"Detective Christianson."

"Is this a work phone, or your private cell number?"

I could hear the exasperation in his voice. "What do you want, Mimi?"

"That Irma lady called. She said to get back to the barn right away." I loved being the messenger.

"What the fuck? She called you?" Exasperation didn't quite describe his voice now.

"Don't kill the messenger. Jeez. She said she was afraid of you. And with an attitude like that, I don't blame her."

"Where are you?" Nick asked warily.

"In my car. Why?" I sure as hell wasn't going to tell him I was on my way to the candle barn.

"Stay put, Mimi. I'll take care of it from here."

I didn't say anything and disconnected.

My phone rang. It was Nick. I let it ring. Oh, boy, was I going to be in a world of hurt.

CHAPTER 18

How Charles was able to get to the barn before me was a secret he'd never share. But his Spyder was sitting in Irma's driveway. I pulled up behind it and got out. I went around to the passenger side and let Lola out, too.

"Why did you bring her?" Charles rubbed between her ears.

"She was with me when I got the call." I held Lola tight on the leash and let her know this was all business.

"Weren't you at home?"

"No." Shit was going to hit the fan when I told this story.

"Mimi?" Charles sounded admonishing, but he was just nosy.

"Fine. I took Lola to visit with Leonard." I took a step back. I knew he wouldn't yell, considering the situation, but I thought for sure he'd get in my face.

"Brilliant! Why didn't I think of that?" He squatted down and rubbed Lola's ears. "So what did you find, my little darling?"

"Nothing. That shithead put a gun in my face," I said.

Charles jumped to stand in front of me. "What? Mimi, you went alone? That was stupid. I thought you went back with Nick. What the hell were you thinking?"

"I certainly didn't think Leonard was a nut job that was going to pull a gun on me. I was thinking Lola might smell something from Tiffany in that house."

"I'm guessing he didn't even let you in the damn house."

A light flickered, and we both turned.

"Who's there?" Irma asked.

"Irma, it's Mimi and Charles," I whispered.

"I told you to come alone." She flashed the light in my eyes.

"No, you didn't." Crazy lady.

"It's okay Irma, I'm just here to be sure Mimi doesn't get hurt." Charles used his most compassionate tone.

"It's Mrs. Tucker to you."

I saw Charles flip her the bird and nearly choked on a giggle.

"Irma, what's going on?" I moved to her side, out of the flashlight's glare.

"There's movement down there. I saw people in the barn, but no cars." She shined the light across the road.

"Mrs. Tucker, aren't you afraid you're going to scare whoever it is off with that light?"

She swung the light around into Charles' face. "What do I give a shit? They're trespassing on my property."

"Well then, why aren't you down there with your fucking shotgun then?" Oh, Charles had had enough of this old bat.

"Do I look like I can handle that shotgun and this flashlight at the same time, you idiot?" She hit him in the arm with the light.

Before she knew what was happening, Charles had taken the flashlight from her grip and turned it on her. "You aren't a very nice old lady. And if I was you, I'd watch very carefully every time I crossed the street from here on out."

Irma Tucker took a step forward and got right in Charles's face. "Fine. You hold the light and I'll go get my shotgun."

I finally stepped in. "No, don't bother. I have Lola here, and she'll guide us in. Charles is probably carrying his Walther PPK anyway." I looked at him. "Right?"

Charles gave Irma back her light, whipped out his gun and a smaller flashlight. "We're good. Let's go."

I led the way across the road, holding Lola close at hand. I stopped and handed the leash to Charles. "Hold her a minute."

I went back to my Land Rover. In the backseat, I scrambled for Tiffany's skirt. Maybe this was a better use of Lola's abilities, anyway. I closed and locked the car, then took the leash back from Charles.

Lola obediently sat, every muscle prepared to launch. I looked both ways on the road, put the skirt to Lola's nose, said, "Lola, suchen," and unsnapped the leash.

Lola dashed across the yard like a shadow, sniffing and following a trail. I took the light from Irma and followed Lola's path with the light. I lost her when she went around the far side of the barn. I didn't even wait for approval from Irma and Charles before dashing across the road to find her. Lola was my baby, and I'd be damned if I was going to let her out of my sight.

I sprinted across the asphalt road and slid across the gravel on the shoulder of the other side. I went straight down, landing on my butt, and the flashlight went flying. I'm not sure what hurt worse, my butt, the gravel digging into my palms, or my ego. And I didn't have time to think about it, because just then I heard Lola whimper.

Behind me, Charles said, "Holy shit. Lola, you're getting prime rib for a month, you wily coyote."

Abandoning his attempt to help me up, Charles made a mad dash to the barn. I watched his shadow in the dark as I gingerly got to my feet.

Irma grabbed me by the elbow. "You okay?"

I nodded, as if she could see it in the dark. I took a step forward and went right back down. I couldn't believe it. I'd wrenched to my ankle.

"No, you definitely are not okay." The old woman lifted me off the ground like a sack of grain, and hauled my arm up around her shoulders. "And I know you aren't going to be happy just waiting here. I sure as hell ain't. Let's see what's going on."

Irma Tucker hauled my butt down that driveway toward the barn like an Olympic weightlifter. We reached the doors just as Charles was poised to ram them open. I could hardly believe the pace at which Irma moved, heaving my (not too tiny) frame along with her.

I saw Charles come to an abrupt stop right before slamming into the door. The outdoor light came on, and I watched Bridget Garrison walk out the door with Tiffany Anderson.

I slumped to the ground, taking poor Irma with me. I was exhausted, hurting like hell, and relieved at the same time. Tiffany was alive.

"Stop right there." The voice came from behind me, but I saw Charles in front of me with his weapon pointed at Bridget. I twisted around to see Nick standing there with his weapon pointed at Charles. Piper had her gun leveled at Bridget.

No one moved. Tiffany looked like a deer in the headlights. Bridget stood frozen. Charles never wavered, his gun still pointed at Bridget's head.

"Charles, put the gun down," Nick said, as he walked toward them.

"Nope. I've got a better shot than you do. I'll put it down when you get here next to me." Charles never looked away from his target.

Nick dropped his gun to his side and sprinted down the driveway. When he was within steps of Charles, he raised his gun again, and Charles dropped his.

In all of this, Lola never left her spot by the door. Charles said, "Lola, comen se bitte."

His German sucked, but Lola understood what he meant. She immediately stood and trotted to him. Charles grabbed her collar and she jumped up in his arms. Now there was a sight, the dapper Charles holding an eighty-pound Doberman while she licked his face. But who was he to complain? She'd done her job better than we could.

I'd never been so proud of my baby. I just wished Dominic could have been here to see what an incredible dog she turned out to be.

The spectacle only lasted a moment, before Charles put her down. He said, "Tiffany? Do you like dogs?"

Tiffany smiled. "Yes." She approached with caution, then bent down and patted Lola on the head. Lola pushed her face at Tiffany, begging for more petting.

"Bridget, what's going on here?" Nick's gun was still aimed at the woman.

"I can explain." She raised her hands in a show of resignation. "I'm not going anywhere. You can put the gun down."

Piper came down the hill and took Bridget's hands down one at a time, putting them in handcuffs behind her back. She walked her away from the barn.

Charles had Tiffany, who was holding Lola's leash, and headed in the same direction.

All seemed quiet for the moment, and the collective sigh of relief was almost audible. Then there was a noise inside the barn, and in a flash, everyone was on alert again.

Stephanie walked out with her hands in the air. "It's just me. I don't have a white flag to wave."

Nick aimed his gun at Stephanie and approached her slowly. "Stephanie, don't make any moves. I'm going to put my gun away and handcuff you."

She only nodded.

Nick gently put the cuffs on Stephanie.

Suddenly, Tiffany let go of Lola's collar and ran after them. "Wait."

Irma Tucker grabbed the girl by the collar of her navy t-shirt. "Hold up there a minute, young lady. Let the police do their job."

Dressed in a t-shirt and jeans that looked a bit too small, Tiffany struggled against Irma's grip. "Let go of me, old lady."

Irma, not taking kindly to being called an old lady, lifted Tiffany a few inches off the ground. "Didn't your momma teach you no manners?"

Charles ran up to Irma. "I've got her."

From where I sat, I said, "Be cool, Irma. This girl has been through a lot."

Nick handed Stephanie off to a uniformed officer and came back down the driveway with a woman I'd never seen.

He walked up to Charles and Tiffany. "Tiffany, I'm Detective Christianson, and this is Nancy Waller. She's from Child Protective Services, and she's going to take you home."

Tiffany's body went limp. "I can't go home," she sobbed. "They'll kill me."

Charles dropped to his knees. "Who's going to kill you, honey?"

I thought I knew the answer, and I'm pretty sure Charles did, too.

Tiffany sniffed. "My parents."

Nancy Waller, a plump woman of about forty, said, "No one is going to kill you, Tiffany. We're going to take you to a safe place until we can talk to your parents. Are you up for that?"

Looking more like a four-year-old than a fourteen-year-old, Tiffany walked away with Nancy.

Nick, Charles, Irma and I watched as they disappeared in the night.

I knew that'd be the last I ever saw of Tiffany Anderson. Somehow I knew her parents would put their would put their house up for sale, and move to a city where no one knew them or what had happened to their daughter.

Nick looked down at me. "What the hell? Get up, let's go."

I whimpered. "I can't." I pointed to my ankle.

CHAPTER 19

I can't say that Nick was the world's greatest nurse, but he sure tried.

It was decided that Lola would go home with Charles, and I'd get a ride to the hospital from Nick. How my car eventually got home, I have no idea.

The sun had risen on a new day when Nick finally made it back to the hospital to pick me up. I'd broken my ankle, but not too badly, just a chip off the medial malleolus. Or, as the doctor explained, the boney bump on the inside of my ankle.

Instead of taking me home, he brought me to his house, where he'd already set up his guest bedroom for my stay. He and Charles had been to my house to pick up some clean clothes, and anything "personal" I might need. After depositing me in bed he left the room and came back with a tray bearing a huge box of donuts (glazed, and cake with sprinkles, my favorite) and a Starbucks peppermint/white chocolate latte, which he sat it on the middle of the bed.

He carefully lay on the bed beside me and handed me the latte. "I heard donuts and coffee have amazing healing powers."

I was starving, but not for food. I wanted to know what transpired while I was at the hospital.

"Can you tell me a story while I eat?"

Nick shook his head, but said, "Bridget had been at William's house that day. Crissy had left her backpack there, and she'd gone back to get it."

"The Twilight backpack?"

"Actually, it was Hello Kitty. When William didn't answer the door, she figured he was at work. She had a key and let herself in."

Listening to Nick's words, I could almost have said them for him. What came next hurt worse than my ankle.

"Just as she grabbed for the backpack, she heard a noise down the hall and went to check, since she thought no one was home. She said the worst thing she expected was to catch her husband having sex with another woman."

I swallowed hard, and put down my donut.

"What she saw was William in the process of trying to rape Tiffany."

My bite of donut was starting to come up. Nick took my hand and held it tight.

"William was on top of Tiffany, with his pants around his ankles. Tiffany was crying and struggling to get out from under him. Bridget said before she knew what she was doing, she'd grabbed a crystal archery trophy he kept on his dresser and smashed in his head."

I wanted to say, "Good for her," but I kept my mouth shut.

"When William rolled off Tiffany, the girl scrambled out of the room. She went to the bathroom to throw up. That's what the mess was."

"So she got away without being raped?"

"Yes, but she'll need counseling." Nick sounded sad.

"Counseling is a good thing."

"Absolutely." He took a donut and took a huge bite. Swallowing, he continued. "When Bridget saw the rage in William's face, she knew he was going to attack her, so she just kept bludgeoning him. She said she had no idea how many times she'd hit him before she remembered Tiffany."

"Was she still in the bathroom?"

"She was gone. That's when Bridget panicked. She searched the house, but couldn't find her. When she went outside, she saw the girl walk into Leonard's house."

I sat straight up in bed. "That fucker. I knew he had something to do with this all along."

"It was his idea to keep the girl, since she was the only witness. He and Bridget took Tiffany to the candle barn."

My head was ready to explode with rage. "That's kidnapping."

"The plan was just to keep her until she calmed down, so they could explain that Bridget was using self-defense when she killed William. Basically, they all panicked." Nick picked up my latte and took a long sip.

"Why did they keep her?"

"The girl was more terrified of what was going to happen when her parents found out than she was of the murder. She begged them to keep her longer, so her parents would be relieved and not pissed."

I was skeptical. "And you believe that?"

"It's not for me to decide. It's for the courts." Nick chewed on the half of a glazed donut he'd stuffed in his mouth.

"Courts? So what are the charges?" Curiously, I'd had it in my mind that there would be no charges.

Relieved to know that everyone was okay, I could feel the pain meds kicking in, and my eyelids grew heavy. I heard Nick say something about second-degree murder, or a plea or something, and I vaguely remembered hearing the words accessory and kidnapping.

Not sure if I was loopy from the pain meds, or the night without sleep, but as I drifted off, I thought I heard Nick say something about staying with him for at least a few days, until I was better.

When I came to, there was some sort of party going on in Nick's house. Still a bit groggy, I could only hear muffled words and familiar voices. Not one to be left out of a party, I grabbed the cane Nick had put next to the bed in case I had to go to the bathroom, and hobbled into the dining room.

Finally, Nick had gotten someone to open a bottle of wine. Several bottles, in fact.

Jackie was the first to see me. "It's about time you join us."

"What's going on?" I looked around to see Catey, Corey, Gemma, Charles, Piper and Nick, too.

Charles raised his glass in a toast. "We're celebrating a new day!"

Piper pushed Charles aside. "I got my permanent assignment." She looked over at Nick, who was toasting with a bottle of Pellegrino. "Nick is going to be my partner for good."

Nick took a swig of the sparkling water, "Or for as long as she can stand me."

Some things just feel better than painkillers. Knowing that Nick's female partner had absolutely no interest in him was one of them.

Nick came over to me, and offered his arm to help me walk to the barstool. "And someone else is getting a new partner, too."

Gemma stuck her hand in my face. "See." She flashed me a two-carat diamond engagement ring. "I'm getting married."

My heart swelled. I knew that for all of Gemma's teasing and flirting, she wanted to settle down. It was finally happening. I realized I'd never been introduced to her boyfriend, nor did I know she had one.

"I'm so happy for you," I slurred. "But I didn't even know you were serious."

"Honey, if a multimillionaire from Dubai wants to marry me, I don't have to be serious." Gemma danced like a racehorse going to the starting gate.

"Before you set a date, let me sober up, so we can talk." Even in my drug-induced haze, I knew this couldn't be good.

Jackie leaned over and whispered, "Just let her be happy for the moment."

I nodded.

"You missed most of the party, but we still have a little something left." Charles held a glass of wine out to me, then switched hands just as I reached out and handed me a bottle of sparkling water. "No drugs and alcohol. Very bad."

I didn't even grab for the bottle, but I wanted to take it from Charles and hit him across the head with it. But he was just being Charles.

Everyone migrated to the living room, where there was ample seating. Catey and Corey were entertaining themselves, texting on their phones. So as long as there was soda and snacks, they were good.

Jackie sat next to me. I leaned over and asked, "Did Anna ever call Catey?"

"Actually, Anna and Crissy are staying with us for a few days, while Bridget and Stephanie get their affairs in order." Jackie looked across at Catey, who seemed oblivious.

"That's interesting."

"They're best friends. Anna explained everything to Catey. She also told her that she's going to be starting therapy sessions next week. Catey has offered to go with Anna as moral support."

What a thoughtful kid Catey was. "Now that's a good friend." Then I thought about Tiffany and asked, "Have you heard anything about Tiffany?"

"Nothing. I drove by her parents' home, but all the drapes were drawn, and there wasn't even a car in the driveway. They picked her up last night, and from what Piper said, it was a tearful reunion. I hope they're understanding about what happened. Piper told me what she said when you found her."

"Once again, I'm reminded how hard it is to be a parent." There was an aching, but it was in my heart, not my ankle.

"And they just let anyone who is willing to have sex have them." Jackie shook her head. This was a soapbox we'd been on many times.

Nick approached and leaned in close. "Come on, you need to go back to bed." He wrapped his arms around my middle and pulled me up from the couch.

Damn if his muscles didn't make me feel all warm and fuzzy. I was hoping this was the beginning of the "one day at a time" thing he'd mentioned before.

"Sorry people, but Mimi needs her rest. I can't have her sleeping in my guest room forever. I'm a bachelor, you know. Puts a mighty big cramp in my style to have a chick living in my house." Nick winked at me.

As I stood there, everyone came over to give me a hug. When Charles hugged me, I asked, "So, was he really going to Paris?"

Charles stood back and looked at me, then at Nick and said, "Why would you even care?" Then he kissed me on the cheek and said his goodbyes. Just before he got to the door, he said, "I think I heard him say something about bringing home real champagne."

I tried not to let it show, but inside, I smiled.

When Catey came to hug me, there were tears in her eyes. "I'm so sorry about all of this, Aunt Mimi." She hugged me tight.

I patted her hair and said, "If it hadn't been for you, we may never have found Tiffany."

She wouldn't look me in the eye. "I guess."

"Just remember this for the next time you meet some cute guy online. Promise?"

"Promise." She sounded so young.

Nick bent down and scooped me up. "It's easier than having you lean on me."

Once we were back in the guest bedroom, I asked, "Why was everyone here at your house?"

"One showed up to see how you were doing, then like some sort of freak magnetic energy field, they all showed up." He leaned over and deposited me in the bed. "This is not how I pictured you in my bed all these months."

He kissed me on the forehead, then handed me a glass of water and another pain pill.

I tossed the pill to the back of my mouth and drank the entire glass. Then settled in for a nap.

Nick sat beside me on the bed. "Want some company until you fall asleep?"

I tried not to grin, but I'm sure I looked like a schoolgirl with a crush. "Sure."

Nick kicked off his shoes, went around to the other side of the bed and climbed under the covers.

As I drifted off to sleep, I swear I heard him say, "One day at a time, Mimi." Then he kissed me softly on the cheek.

And now an excerpt from *Death of a Sales Rep*

CHAPTER 1

Sometimes the best parts of life are the times you get to screw with another person's head. It's not so great when someone is fucking with yours, but whoever said life was fair? So cliché, but then I spy on cheating spouses--and cheats in general--for a living. My life is a cliché.

I start most every day by heading to work at the detective agency I own. I started Gotcha Detective Agency a few years back, when my life fell apart and I needed something to keep me focused on living. If you believe the hype, I'm living the American dream. I own my own business, my own house, and I have a dog. And according to the insurance company, I also have a husband. Dominic, my husband, died a few years ago, but since the body was never recovered from the wreckage of the plane, the insurance company still considers me to be married. I don't wear my wedding ring anymore, mostly because it leaves a tan line, and I don't want my target on a decoy job to know I'm married.

As I eased into my parking space, I looked up to see one of my business partners waiting. Lola, my Doberman, saw him too, and leapt out of the car in record speed.

"You ready to go?" Charles asked, as he opened my door and petted Lola simultaneously.

I'm Mimi Capurro, and Charles Parks is my right hand man. And to be honest, he's my left hand,

and many times he's my feet too. That is, when he's not tripping me up like this morning.

"Baby, I was born ready." Actually, I had no idea what the hell Charles was talking about. "But can you remind me exactly what I was born ready for?"

I followed Charles up the back stairs and into the kitchen, Lola between us. Gotcha's offices are in an old Victorian house that used to be the offices of Dominic's produce brokerage business. Most of the rooms have been converted to offices, but we kept the kitchen and the two luxurious bathrooms too.

I knew he wasn't planning a day at the agency, as he wore burnt umber pants rolled at the ankles, and an untucked cream V-neck tee. Not his normal "fop" work attire. His tan sneakers squeaked on the hardwood floor as he straightened and cleaned the room. I knew he was mad. Just as Lola grabbed a mouthful of food when she was scolded, Charles cleaned when pissed off.

"I'll ask again, ready for what?" I snatched the coffee cup from Charles' hand.

"San Francisco," he snapped.

San Francisco? Then the light bulb went on. San Francisco! I cleaned and rinsed the coffee cup while facing the sink, so Charles couldn't see the panic on my face. "Well, crap, you'd think with as much as you've babbled on about it, I'd have remembered. Are you sure it's this weekend?"

I had promised to go to San Francisco to support Charles' friend, Anthony DeLuca, at his first trade show. Anthony made a highly sought after line of voodoo dolls. *I know, right?* It's amazing how many people bought his high-end voodoo toy.

Anthony had recently fired his sales rep and was now selling the dolls himself. In the six years he'd been manufacturing the dolls, he'd never had to design a booth and sell for himself. He'd always had sales reps, but after one greedy rep filed a suit against him for firing her, he decided he'd be in charge of his own fate. Funny enough, his business soared. Turned out, Anthony wasn't the only person who didn't care for the sales rep's pushy ways.

"So your bag is packed?" Before I could answer, Charles added, "I'll just go out and get it for you."

"I have my overnight bag in my car. Besides, I probably won't be staying the night. I don't have a sitter for Lola."

I always kept an overnight bag handy, for stakeouts, and whatever else might come up. Not that anything else ever did come up. The bag held a couple of changes of clothes, that little black dress for every occasion, a week's worth of underwear, flats, athletic shoes, and pumps, and all of the toiletries and makeup a girl might need in any situation. You never know…

"Jackie will be here to get her," he looked at his watch, "in about an hour."

Jackie Bacarrin was one of my detectives, and my best friend. One of the last cases I'd worked on involved her daughter, Catey. It was a true lesson in paying attention to who your children were interacting with online.

"What?" Charles had once again taken over my life. Don't get me wrong, I appreciated it when I wanted him there, but this was all about him now. "Okay, San Francisco aside, we have an important conference call this morning," I said, as I wiped out the coffee cup and poured coffee into it.

Charles whipped out his phone and looked at the

calendar. "Oh, shit, the Hewes Chemical Management account. That conference call is today?" He headed to the front of the building.

If we could land the Hewes Chemical account, we could put a huge notch in our belt. Hewes was one of the largest corporate accounts we'd ever had the chance to land. Usually, with corporations, it's a case of workman's comp or disability fraud, but this one was about much more. Not that we could go around bragging about the case, confidentiality and all, but we'd be able to refer to it without names. It'd look good on a business resume.

"Nine o'clock, dear," I said, as I trailed him.

"Just one more thing about San Francisco, then I'll drop it until after the meeting." Charles looked over his shoulder at me.

I resigned myself. "What?"

"I invited Nick to come help out."

Now that stopped me in my tracks. In a million years I'd never have guessed.

Not once, in all the chatter about the trip to San Francisco, did Charles mention he'd invited him. It pissed me off that the sound of Nick's name had my heart nearly pounding through my chest. Part of me was excited as hell that he'd be there, but it'd been weeks since we'd talked, and the other part of me dreaded seeing him.

Nick Christianson and I had been taking it one day at a time since the last case we'd been thrown together on. I knew down to my core that I wanted it to be more, but I wasn't going to wear my heart on my sleeve just to have it ripped to shreds again. I didn't think I could handle that. It seemed that one day at a time kept turning into two days, then two weeks to the point where we didn't have time for each other.

"Charles, can I talk to you for a minute?" I called after him.

The pompous ass completely ignored me. I wanted to know why on earth he'd ask Nick to come along. It wasn't like Charles and Nick were friends. Sure, they'd done business together. Nick was a cop and Charles did freelance work for the police, so their paths crossed. Charles' skills as a computer forensics tech were renowned, and the Salinas Police Department seemed to be using his services more often. Even the drug dealers and gangs had gotten into the digital age, and Charles was there to thwart them whenever possible.

What miffed me the most was that Charles hadn't told me he'd been in touch with Nick. He usually loved to rub that stuff in my face.

Nick's one of the Salinas Police Department's homicide detectives. He also happened to be my old college fling. Until earlier this year, when we were reunited on a murder case, I hadn't seen him in--um--a couple of years. (Whew, I almost dated myself.)

My thoughts turned from Nick to Lola, as she stopped at the reception desk. The hairs on her back stood on end, as if attracted to a magnet, and her growl was low and menacing.

Charles snapped his fingers and Lola dropped to the ground, but still on high alert. When I caught up to him, I looked across the reception desk to see a vaguely familiar face. It was Cortnie Criss, my new employee.

Cortnie had been an associate of Charles' when they worked together at the Naval Postgraduate School, and he had recommended her when a position became available with our agency. She stood there, all five foot four of her, not the least bit intimidated by Lola. I guess with her black pumps, she actually stood about five seven, and she looked fit in her black pencil skirt, bare legs, and a fitted black T-shirt. She had classic good looks that required only a bit of blush and possibly some mascara to look beautiful.

She'd been training for a few days, but this was the first time our agency mascot was being introduced.

"Lola, meet Cortnie." He gestured to Lola, who rose to a sitting position and lifted her paw as if to shake. "Cortnie, Lola. I'm sure you two will become fast friends, because Lola loves everyone I love, and darling, I just love you."

Cortnie wasn't stupid enough to approach Lola and shake her paw. She looked down at the Doberman and smiled. "Pleased to meet you, Lola. I hope we will be friends." She looked at Charles, "She's not going to rip me to shreds, is she?"

Charles handed Cortnie a liver treat. "Step out here." Cortnie did as instructed. "Now put the treat in the palm of your hand and hold it there with your thumb."

Cortnie did as Charles said, and Lola's growl turned to a whimper.

"Okay, turn your hand palm down and raise it to shoulder level."

Cortnie complied, not at all hesitant.

"Meet Lola, your new best friend. Just say, 'Lola, touch.'"

Cortnie said, "Lola, touch."

Lola leapt from her sitting position and snagged the treat from Cortnie's palm. It was a swift, yet gentle movement, and I had to give her credit for not flinching. She obviously trusted Charles implicitly.

Charles turned and looked at me. "See, I told you Cortnie was a gem."

The phone rang just then, and Cortnie answered it. Lola trotted over to her and rested her chin on Cortnie's lap. All was good in the Gotcha Detective Agency world.

"One moment, please." Cortnie put the call on hold. "It's Richard Clinton from HCM."

"I've got it." I rushed to my office, grabbing Charles by the arm.

"I don't need to be there. I've briefed Cortnie on everything she needs to know. She'll be fine." He stood his ground.

"Charles, you are sitting in on this call. It won't last that long and you're the expert with the technology we'll be using."

Charles grabbed Cortnie's hand. "You need to join us. This is the case you've been reading about. We'll probably be using your surveillance equipment."

Cortnie grabbed her iPad ® and joined us in my office.

I pressed the speaker button on my phone. Mr. Clinton got right to the point.

"I wanted to let you know that I've talked to our board, and we've decided to listen to your plan of attack." He sounded much younger than his sixty-five years.

Clinton was the president of Hewes Chemical Management, or HCM Incorporated, a national chemical company. He suspected that chemicals were missing from his local warehouses and was considering using our agency for surveillance.

I looked at Charles, who knew the details of the equipment we planned to use, but he just looked back at me. He really wasn't going to participate in this call.

"Mr. Clinton, I have Charles Parks, and another detective, Cortnie Criss, in here with me."

"Hello, Mr. Clinton, I'm Cortnie Criss." She sounded classy and sure of herself, and I liked that.

Cortnie had been hired to replace Gemma, who was a junior detective with our agency. Gemma had found true love and moved across the country, all in a matter of days. Cortnie's expertise was in video surveillance, so this case was right up her alley.

I was pretty sure Charles hadn't had time to get her up to speed on this account, as he hadn't even remembered the call.

"Charles updated me on the situation this morning. So you think your local vice-president is padding his yearly bonus with chemicals from your company?" she said.

"That's one way to put it," Clinton said. "The inventory numbers seem to be fine, but the barrels in the warehouse don't seem to match the numbers on the page. Then, when I mentioned it, the barrels were suddenly there again. So I dropped the inquiry, hoping that with enough time I'd see another discrepancy. Last week, something was off again."

"From what I have here," Cortnie looked at her iPad®, tapped and slid her fingers across the screen, then looked up. "It's been six months since the first inquiry."

"Yes, that's correct."

"So, the chemical in question is methylamine chloride? Mr. Clinton, you know what this chemical is used for, right?"

I sucked in my breath. Did she really just ask the president of an international chemical company if he knew what his product was used for?

"Ms. Criss, I know exactly what it's used for." He didn't sound miffed, or insulted. "I also know what it's used for illegally."

"I just wanted to be sure we were on the same page. I understand that you know its use in pesticides, pharmaceuticals, and such. Now I know you know it's used to make methamphetamine, too."

"I just don't know who would be stealing it from my warehouses. My employees are very well compensated. I don't see why any of them would have a need to supplement their income with illegal activities."

We all looked at each other and rolled our eyes. People in high places could be so naïve. It's human nature to be greedy; enough is never enough. And the person the world sees may not be the real deal. I'm constantly amazed at what people do behind closed doors.

"One can never be sure of another's motives, sir." Cortnie typed on her iPad ®.

"We can't let anyone in the facility know that we are investigating, correct?" I asked.

"I'm just not sure who I can trust, so no." Clinton sounded tense.

"That's not a problem. We can go to the facility late at night and set up our equipment. No one needs to know we were there," Cortnie offered.

"And how do you expect to get in?" Clinton inquired.

Cortnie was nonplussed. "We can break in, or you can provide us with entry. There is always a way to bypass the security system and not let anyone know the perimeter has been breached."

"You sound like someone I wouldn't want to cross." Mr. Clinton's voice was a bit less strained.

"Who, me?" Cortnie laughed. "All in a day's work. I'd never use my skills for personal gain."

"When would you like us to start?" I asked.

"The sooner, the better. I just have to figure a way to get you past our security. We have doormen, and video twenty-four seven." The edge in Mr. Clinton's voice bothered me.

"No problem. I'll go in late tonight or early in the morning. I just need a copy of the building's floor plan. Can you email them to me in an attachment?" Cortnie knew her stuff.

"I'll have my assistant do that right away."

"Can your assistant be trusted?" I inquired.

"Absolutely. I'm going to tell her it's for a possible expansion. Do you have a personal email, not the agency one, that I can give her?"

Cortnie gave him her personal email address, and said, "Perfect. I'll look over the plans, and I'll need the information about the security in the building, so I can figure out how to bypass it. The sooner you get this to me, the better prepared I'll be." Cortnie looked at me and smiled.

"We'll also need personnel files. We'll need to look into the background of your employees at that location. Are the files digital?" I said.

"I don't know how I'll get that to you. If I have my assistant do it, she'll be suspicious. I trust her, but she doesn't have access to the human resources files."

Cortnie said, "Human resources can be told that we are doing a labor audit. I can send a formal letter, but usually, there is a long period of time between the notification and the audit."

"We can call HR and tell them we are inquiring as to why we haven't received the files yet, claiming we sent the request more than a month ago." I was thinking aloud.

"No, I'll do it," Clinton said. "If you can dummy up some paperwork, I'll run it to HR and tell them my assistant brought it to my attention. I'll ask that the files be sent to me, and I'll forward them."

"It's not normal protocol, but we can try to make it work," Cortnie said. "Of course, all of this will take some time."

"Mr. Clinton, this is Charles Parks. Cortnie is one of the developers of the equipment we'll be using to investigate, which is state of the art. Most P.I. agencies couldn't afford this quality, but we are lucky to have the equipment and the developer. You're in good hands."

"Thank you so much, Mr. Parks."

"Mr. Clinton, may I ask, what made you decide to choose Gotcha Detective Agency? There are plenty of agencies closer to San Francisco." Something about this case bothered me.

"Oh, believe me, Ms. Capurro, I've spent the last six months doing my homework, and you come very highly recommended."

Charles glared at me as if to say, "Are you trying to ruin this?"

Cortnie saved the moment. "Mr. Clinton, I'm going to put you on hold for just a moment while I go back to my desk. I want to get a little more information from you. Is that okay?"

He agreed, and Cortnie stood to leave.

"Great job, Cortnie. I hope we can pull it off as well as you described it."

Cortnie smiled. She had a genuine smile with beautiful, not quite perfect teeth, and I saw warmth in it. "We'll do better than just pull it off. This is my forte. I couldn't have started working for you at a better time."

"I have to agree. So glad to have you."

As we were saying our goodbyes, my breath caught, because Nick was standing in the doorway. Charles looked to see what I was gawking at, grinned, and left the room.

I pulled myself together and went to greet him. Not much I could do about how I looked, though I did want to do a butt check as I walked around the desk. Did I look too fat in these pants? No, I'd be okay; it's why I wear black.

How many weeks had it been? Nick looked as good as the last time I saw him: his black hair, just a bit long with unruly waves, the twinkle in his gray eyes when he smiled, and the way he wore khakis and a polo shirt made me want to jump him. But I was going to be cool, way too cool, and never let him know just how good he looked.

"Damn, my man, don't you look hot in Thursday casual?" Charles nearly drooled.

I guess I didn't have to tell him just how good he looked after all. Charles did it for me.

Nick looked at me and smiled. From his face, you'd think we'd just spoken yesterday. It was familiar and friendly. Mine, on the other hand, was not. He'd let one day at a time turn into one week at a time, and I was still waiting to see where we were headed after a few weeks.

I had to be realistic where Nick was concerned. We'd never been very good in the relationship department, at least not with each other. In college, we hooked up for a good time, or to lick our wounds from other relationships that had gone bad. My core heated just at the thought of having sex with Nick. We'd been good in bed. Not that we ever used a bed. Oh, wait, did I say that? We may have used a bed once or twice. I'm not promiscuous, but I *am* weak where that man is concerned. He could probably talk me into cheating on my spouse, if I had one.

"You look good as always," Nick said, looking at me.

Charles answered, "Thanks."

Nick rolled his eyes.

"Yes, Charles does look good, doesn't he? And thank you." I laughed. It was going to be a long day, so I'd better make the best of it.

"I'm ready when you are." Nick was definitely addressing Charles this time.

"Sweet. I have my bags packed and in my car." Charles then snapped at me, "Ready?"

"You're sure this won't interfere with our surveillance tonight?" With Charles, everything was on his agenda, not mine.

"Positive. You're just helping set up and if there's time, we can go to the hospitality party."

I walked out to the reception desk. "Cortnie, is there anything I can do for you before we leave?"

"No, I think I have everything I need. If I have any questions, I'll give you a call."

"You have a bag packed?" Nick asked me.

"I always have a bag packed." I looked pointedly at Charles. "Will you excuse me?"

I went to the kitchen to rinse out my coffee cup and put it in the sink. Just then, Lola appeared in the room. I opened the pantry and grabbed the bag of dog food. Lola liked the small kibbles, not the big dog chunks. I poured a heaping cup into her dish next to the refrigerator, patted her on the head and said, "Don't be too much of a pain for Jackie." She grabbed a mouthful and trotted off to leave little piles of dog food around the house.

Jackie hadn't arrived for work yet, but she was used to taking Lola for a couple of days at a time. This was perfect, because Jackie's twins loved Lola, and she loved them. They'd watch Lola even if Jackie had a stakeout.

I heard Nick yelling from the front of the house. "Hey, Mimi, let's go."

"Ugh," I said, quietly. Thank goodness I'd have an hour and a half during the drive to chastise Charles for inviting Nick. He'd be sorry by the time we reached the convention center.

Once there, we'd help Anthony set up and evaluate his booth. Then he wanted to do a run through and take some mock orders to be sure he was getting all the right information. When we had dinner last week, I'd never seen Anthony so nervous. He was really worried about running his own booth for the first time.

I grabbed my car keys from the kitchen table, where I'd dropped them when I arrived. I yelled back, "I'll meet you in the parking lot."

As I headed to my Land Rover and checked the contents of my overnight bag, Nick's Porsche Boxster turned into the lot.

Charles grabbed my bag. "Oh, by the way, you'll be riding with Nick. Leave the keys in your car so Cortnie can use it." He turned away from me quickly, so he didn't see the look on my face. He tossed my bag into the back of Nick's Boxster, and said, "Come on. Let's get a move on."

My heart thudded in my chest as I opened the door and got in the car with Nick.

…end of excerpt

About the Author

A native of Northern California, Jamie was swept off her feet by a dashing farm boy and transplanted to Iowa. And after several years of running a restaurant with her husband, she felt the urge to kill people. I mean she decided to start writing mysteries. Let Us Prey is the first in her Gotcha Detective Agency Mysteries series.

Her short script, No One Knows, produced by Daniel Hoyos and directed by Bunee Tomlinson, was filmed in August 2012 and is now an award winning short film, as it won its category at Bare Bones Film Festival.

With 3 novels in the Gotcha Detective Mystery Series, *Let Us Prey* (an Amazon Mystery Series bestseller), *Textual Relations*, and *Death of a Sales Rep,* she's working on the 4th, called *What a Meth*, and polishing 3 feature screenplays which she's written. Jamie prides herself in working on several projects at a time, so she's never bored.

Jamie is a novelist and screenwriter, writing for both features and television. She is co-founder of Scriptchat on Twitter http://www.scriptchat.com & TVWriterChat http://www.tvwriterchat.com, and is the former president of RWA's screenwriting chapter, <u>Script Scene</u>.

Jamie still lives in Iowa (though she visits California as often as possible) with her husband, 2 dogs, 2 cats and 3 horses. She writes with a view from her 6 acre farm.

Connect with Jamie Online:

Website: http://www.jamieleescott.com

Twitter http://www.twitter.com/authorJamie

Facebook Fan Page:
http://www.facebook.com/jamie.jld

12987916R00129

Made in the USA
San Bernardino, CA
03 July 2014